CLEO BROWNE

Judge

Devil's Rose MC Book Seven

Contents

Trigger Warning

This book deals with badassery in all its forms.
Please be aware that in order for these characters to be badass,
this book contains content that some readers may find
disturbing,
such as graphic descriptions of violence and torture, and R18
sex scenes.

Hey Readers!

Well, this is one that almost killed me.

Not because the story was so emotional or fraught, but because it happens at the same time as Marx's timeline and that's always a tricky one to deal with. Why did I plan it like this? Well, I didn't. We can all blame Marx for jumping the queue and pushing poor old Judge down the line. Anyhoo, his happy ending (heh) has been happening in the background, so here it is.

Enjoy.

C

Who the heck is that?

Devil's Rose MC

Marx - Pres + Lovely
= Bee
Rhodie - VP and Enforcer + Tuesday Tombs (Chewy) Icer
= Laney May
Rider - SAA
Wire - Secretary/Hacker + Remy Wright
= Jovie (Wire and Remy's adopted child)
Tank - Member + Mira (Doll) Campbell
Switch - Medic
Judge - Road Captain + Kaia
= Jax & Annie-Bella
Sniper - Member
Fox - Member
Nitro - Member
Savage - Member (ex Death Rider) + Nat
= Rosie
Dex - Member (Ex Death Rider)
TumTum (Jimmy) - Member
Chef (Takoda) - Member
Tav - Member + Blanche (Pixie)
= Niko, Sage, Cove, Elio, Tess
Niko - Prospect

Mad Dog – Retired President, Father of Marx and Rhodie

Tombs Security

August (Gus) Tombs + Ana Tombs
= Jr (Sidney)
Jules Tombs + Violet Davies
= Juno
Tav Tombs + Blanche Landry
= Niko, Sage, Cove, Elio, Tess
Tuesday (Chewy) Tombs + Rhodie
= Laney–May
Sidney (Pops) Tombs + Debs Taylor (Mother of Ana)

Bartashev Bratva

Roman Bartashev + Sasha Bartashev (BFF's of Ana)
Dima

Chapter 1

Judge

It's going to be fine. All I have to do is walk into the diner, march up to Kaia, let her know she's in danger and that she needs to come with me. Easy. Simple. There will be no push back, no questions. Kaia will just follow along like a little lamb and smile politely while she does it.

Yeah, right. Kaia will take one look at me and kick me out on my ass. If she doesn't do that, she'll stab me in the eye with a fork. Either way there will be violence. I just know it. I shouldn't be surprised really. I've known Kaia for most of my life. Well, I had known Kaia for most of my life. Before I fucked that up by getting my dick wet with Chelsea Masters, the high school bicycle. Up until that point Kaia and I had fooled around a few times. We had both been awkward as hell, so we wanted to lose our virginities to someone we trusted. The first time sucked. Badly. The second and third time? Well, let's just say that after a decade and a half of fucking easy women, those two times were something that I've never felt since.

Deep breath in, deep breath out. I throw my leg over my

Harley Davidson Roadster, the navy blue tank glistening in the sunlight. Dismounting I stand and take another deep breath. This is going to go badly, and I'll have witnesses. I try to ignore them, but the Girl Gang is all lined up on the pavement like a damned receiving line. I give them a nod as I walk past, because let's face it, if I ignore them they'll give me even more shit to add on to what's going to be a pretty shitty day by anyone's standards. I mean this and then the fact that our club is under attack and we'll be locking down? Yeah, I think I'd prefer to be back out in the sandbox I met Rhodie in, getting shot at.

I take one last deep fortifying breath before stepping up to the door of the diner.

"Yo Boomer! Outta the way!" a kid yells, skidding up next to me on his skateboard, kicking and catching it in one slick movement.

"Who the hell are you calling Boomer?" I grumble but he pays no attention, instead flinging the door open wide enough for him to slip through, but my big ass gets hit on my way in after him.

Fucking youth. There's probably a reason why at the ripe old age of thirty-three I haven't had any children. I'm scary looking. I'm quiet. I'm fucking grumpy. Don't get me wrong, the MC kids and babies are all good, I can smile at them and say hi, but let's just say that I don't see myself with small versions of me any time soon.

"Hi! Can I help you? We have seats around the counter or you can take a table at the back?" A young girl asks from beside my elbow before glancing at the punk, then back at me.

I stare down at her, blinking to try and get my thoughts back together after that fucking teenager set me off kilter. I can see the little bastard now, standing behind the counter smirking at a teen on the other side. As if I needed another reason to avoid this place.

The little brunette stares up at me in anticipation of my answer. "Shit, sorry, um, counter."

"Perfect!" She bounces off with way too much energy, joining that little douche canoe behind the counter. He shoulder bumps her and I get the urge to scare the shit outta him. That's not how you treat women.

Shaking off my already worsening mood, I nod once again at the Girl Gang, this time all of them perched along the counter, with Pops and Mad Dog in tow. Fuck my life. Deciding to just bite the bullet I make my way to the counter, staring down the little skateboard punk.

"Yo, can I help you?" the punk smirks.

"Yeah, you always try to run over customers?"

"I gave you a heads up. Not my fault your reflexes suck." He gives me a sickly sweet smile. "What can I get for you?"

I have no idea how old this kid is, probably because I don't know enough to compare, but I'd say he's a little younger than Sage and Niko. Maybe around early teens but big for his age. He's tall and solidly built, but not old enough to have grown out of the slight gangliness that kids his age have.

Choosing to ignore the little shit I decide to just ask, "Yeah, I'm looking for Kaia."

His brows pull down, eyes flicking to my cut, then back up to my face. "Why?"

My eyes move to the little brunette, standing at his elbow. She's a heck of a lot smaller than he is, but flicking between the two I can see the resemblance in the set of their chins. There's something oddly familiar about these kids, but I'd remember them. Well, the asshole one at least.

3

"Yo, creep, stop staring at my sister." The kid steps in front of the brunette, shielding her.

"Why are you looking for our mom?" his sister asks.

"Annie-Bella, go serve those people down there, I'll take care of this," the boy murmurs, giving his sister a look. She nods once and then heads toward the Girl Gang who have eyes glued in my direction.

"Leo, what the hell are you doing here? I thought I told you that you're barred from my establishment?" Kaia's husky voice barks in my direction.

She's standing in the middle of her diner, hands on her hips, hair wild, looking like fucking Medusa. If her gaze could turn me to stone she would. She'd probably then grind that stone to dust and dance on it. Or take a shit on it.

"Kaia, I need to talk to you. It's urgent," I plead, palms out, as if to implore some soft, sweet part deep inside her.

Instead, she throws her head back and laughs in my face. "No. Nope. Not at all. Doubt it. You need to get gone Leo Jackson. And don't come back." She scowls my way, but I don't miss the way her eyes dart, the way they constantly look past me to the kids working the counter.

There's a flutter in my gut that things aren't quite what I think they are. There was never any explanation about where Kaia went. One day she was there staring at me like I'd ripped her heart out, the next, gone. I tried reaching out and nothing. No word, no letters. Shit, I even created a fucking social media profile to see if I could find her. Then she pops up in my town, an hour away from where we grew up, and bars me from entering her diner. The best fucking diner in town. No, something is up, and I'm going to fucking get to the bottom of it.

I *know* Kaia. I know all her quirks and tells. I also know her

4

weaknesses. So I don't argue. I just watch her. Watch her every move. Watch the way her dark eyes dart to her kids and back. The way she bristles every time I look in their direction. The way she wrings her hands and gives them tight smiles when they begin shooting her concerned glances.

I'm thirty-three years old. Kaia is thirty-two, thirty-three in three weeks. That big annoying kid looks to be maybe thirteen or fourteen? Kaia left when I was eighteen. My gaze shoots to hers, my stomach dropping into my boots.

"Kaia," my voice barely a whisper above the din in the diner. "How old is your son?"

Her eyes widen, dark pools staring directly into my soul, a resigned look on her face. "He's fourteen. They both are."

Kaia

I watch as the father of my children slowly crumples to the floor, the big bastard taking out my waitresses' tray, spilling pancakes and maple syrup onto the floor before his giant ass lands in it.

"Ah, shit kid, come on, let's get you cleaned up." A kind faced older man with the same leather vest Leo wears grips him under the arm while Jax and Annie-Bella come racing over.

"You OK, Mom? Want me to kick that guy's ass?"

A little huff escapes me, "Jax, what have I told you about kicking asses?"

"No need to kick ass when you can use your words," he replies in a bored voice.

"Don't worry, Mom! I have the bucket and mop," Annie-

Bella sloshes water onto the floor where Leo's ass print is proudly on display.

"Baby, I'll do that, you go serve the MC women," I smile gently at her. My little girl is a nurturer.

I have no idea how I managed to raise two completely different people, but I did. Jax is a lot like Leo at the same age. Big, talented at sports, academic at school. The only difference is he got my smart mouth and terrible temper. Annie-Bella is quiet, gentle, also sporty like her brother but her academics starts and ends with reading and writing. She hates math and science, but give her a pen and paper and she can make whole worlds out of nothing but her imagination.

"Um, hi. You probably don't remember me–"

"Of course I do, you're Lovely, right?" I reply immediately.

I know all the women sitting along the countertop. They come in often for mommies group with Pops, Chewy's grand-father. They're a hell of a good time, if not a little nosy. They know all the sordid details of why I don't talk to Leo, or want him anywhere near my diner.

"Oh! Um, yup, that's me." Lovely's pale cheeks pinken a little. I have no idea why she would think I'd forget her. She's got this sort of gentleness about her that you just don't see much. Especially not in women who hang around the MC.

All the women, aside from her and Mira seem to be the type to not take shit from anyone. I quite like that about them, too.

"Um, Judge, if he ever comes out of the bathroom, is going to ask you to accompany him, us, to the farmhouse we are all staying at. I'm not sure if you heard, but the clubhouse was attacked? We're all fine, but the clubhouse is not." Her eyes are wide and she darts them to the bathroom door, then back to me.

My brows pull down in confusion. "Wait, why would I need to go with him?"

"We have reason to believe that the person who did it knows about your connection to Judge."

"Leo. His name is Leo. Well it was when we were young," I mutter. Back when we were inseparable. Best friends. "Besides, we have no connection to each other at all."

She raises her brows, flicking her gaze to the two teens behind the counter. "Really?" Lovely asks, her gaze swinging back to mine.

My blood feels like ice as it pumps through my veins, thumping in my head, "Are you telling me there's a threat to *my* babies and Leo is the reason? Because if that's the case I will cut his balls off with a rusty spoon. It's bad enough what he did, but endangering *my* babies with his life choices? Oh, hell no!"

The door to the bathroom slams open and my gaze is laser focused in that direction. I have no peripheral vision anymore. It's all on the big bastard walking out of the bathroom hall with the gall to look shell-shocked. My feet move me in his direction before I even have the time to think.

"You!" I hiss, finger pointing directly into his stupidly hard looking chest. "Leo-fucking-Jackson, mind telling me what the hell is going on and why the hell there's a bad guy out there thinking we have a connection?"

Leo stares down at me, those damn green eyes I used to dream about filled with confusion. Well he can stick his confusion. I sent email after bloody email to LeoLovesLasagne@hotmail and text messages and never got a reply. So screw him and the horse he rode in on.

He takes a deep breath in. His huge chest, level with my eyeline puffs out like an overinflated air mattress. How much does this guy bench?

"Kaia," he says gently and I want to slap my name out of his mouth. "You're in danger. Your, m-my, *our* kids, are in danger."

"*My* kids, not yours. Mine. Because of you!" I jab him in the chest, just because I can.

His gaze drops to where I jabbed him, and he looks somewhat amused, but I'm not falling for that lopsided grin. He must remember why he came here because he takes *another* deep breath, his shoulders slumping as he exhales. "I don't want to argue with you. But, we have shit going down. I don't know how they knew about you. Or the kids. All I know is they're dangerous and the safest place you can all be, is with the club."

My brows lower. "I thought Lovely said your compound was attacked."

"It was. We're all sheltering at Chewy's place. There's enough room for everyone. You and the kids can have one of the trailers we have on site. I will stay in the big house so you can have your space." He clamps his mouth shut, as if afraid to say anything more.

He should be afraid. Does he not see that after no contact for fourteen years that asking me to pack up *my* kids and trust him and his MC family to look after us is a damn ridiculous request? And yet, we've been in town for a few months and some bad guy has put together our relationship to Leo, no matter how much I wish there wasn't one.

"This threat, it's real?"

"I know it doesn't mean much, but you have my word. The threat is real."

"And they're dangerous?"

His Adam's apple bobs as he swallows. "They destroyed our

clubhouse. They hurt people."

"Shit," I curse under my breath.

My hands fist and I really want to punch Leo. Or something. Anything to make this situation better. It's been a long time since I last relied on a man. That man was my father and he was killed because of it. But what choice do I have? I have a public business, the whole frontage is glass, you can see right in, to everybody dining and whoever is serving on the counter. My stomach drops when I think that whoever it is doing this can probably see my kids going about their daily lives as we speak. Turning and rushing into the main diner room I let out a breath when I see the kids are both busy chatting to customers, Annie-Bella with her hand on an elderly patron's shoulder, Jax with the coffee pot doing refills.

I can feel Leo behind me, his presence heavy, like my heart, but what choice do I have?

"Fine. I'll close down the diner. I have insurance to cover missed wage-"

"We can cover that. The MC will cover all your expenses."

I nod numbly. It'll hurt business having to close, but I need to keep my babies safe. They're all I have in the world, and no one is going to take them from me.

"Fine. I'll do it."

"Thank yo-"

"It's not for you."

Leo nods mutely, his eyes darting over my shoulder at the two people who own my heart. Turning, I catch sight of my son, fiercely standing in front of his sister, a scowl on his face. Annie-Bella peeking around him, a hopeful look on hers. Since she was little she's always wondered why other kids have fathers. I haven't kept anything from them. They know how they came to be, and they know that after my aborted attempt to tell Leo in person, that I tried through phone and email messages. I heard nothing from the man. To think that we've both ended up in the same town at the same time is mind blowing, given that neither of us are from here, instead, from a few towns over. Last I heard he was in the marines or something. Clearly my intel was wrong and now I have to let the kids and my employees know that we're closing the diner for a few days due to a "family emergency". Great.

"I'll take care of everything here and be at the farmhouse later."

"I can-"

"No. I've got this."

Letting out a sigh I paste on a smile and get back to work, ignoring the weight of Leo's gaze on my back as I walk away. I can do this. For the safety of my kids, I have to.

Chapter 2

Judge

"How are you getting on big guy?" Lovely's voice breaks me out of the daze I'm in.

I turn to look down at her pale face, looking a hell of a lot better than the last time I saw her. She almost seems invigorated from the shit her and the Girl Gang got up to maiming cartel members in an alleyway. If you had told me way back when she first arrived that she would be in the thick of things with Chewy and Blanche, I would have laughed in your face. That was until she joined Devil's Big Tow. She not only whipped Tank and I into shape, she also called in the debts and got us all square. She runs the office with an iron fist, and if I'm honest, I have no idea what we did without her. She's got the same grit as the other women, although hers is tempered with softer edges.

Looking at her open, kind face makes me want to tell her exactly how I feel, which is almost unheard of. I'm the guy that only speaks when I have something to say. Which isn't often. It's always been like that, ever since I was in kindergarten.

That's where I met Kaia. She was on the swing, by herself, trying to get the momentum to swing high. She's small now, but she was tiny then. I, on the other hand, was a big fucker. Both my parents are tall and wide, and my father used to tell me that people like us needed to use our size to help people. Taking his advice, I walked up to Kaia and pushed her, without speaking a word. I never had to, she filled in all the gaps, she could read me like nobody else. We shared everything from that day. Until I fucked up. My gut screws up just thinking about it.

"I'm not sure, Lovely. For years I just thought we lost touch. What I did was shitty, but that woman was my best friend. One day she was there, the next she was gone. Packed up, moved out of town. Then all of a sudden she's back, with two kids in tow and she never told me." My shoulders slump as the words leave a bitter taste on my tongue. "Did I really hurt her so bad that she would rather parent twins on her own than tell me?"

Lovely moves a little closer. Not so close that she's touching me, which I appreciate. Just close enough that I can feel the heat of her body next to mine. It's comfortable and comforting, as if Lovely can read me just like Kaia used to.

"You were both young, Judge. I'm sure there's more to the story than you think. The best thing to do would be to talk to her. I know you were best friends once, but you're different people than you were at eighteen. Talk to her, get to know each other again, and open up." She smiles gently at me. "Did she agree to come to the farm?"

"Yeah. But she's pissed about it."

"Well, I would be too," she laughs.

"She said to give her an hour to pack up, and she'll be here."

"Is that why you're standing outside an empty trailer?"

I smirk down at Lovely. She's so good at reading other people, it's hilarious that she can't read Marx in the same way. "That's funny."

She pulls back a little, looking up at me, brows pinched in confusion. "What's funny?"

"You can read the whole situation with me and what I've got going on. Offer advice. Hell, you even figured out why I was standing here, and yet you can't figure out Marx's feelings for you."

She scoffs, digging her toe into the ground, not looking at me. "Marx doesn't feel anything for me. Perhaps gratitude for making sure he wasn't hurt that day, but that's about the extent of it."

My lips tip up even further, into almost a full smile. "If you say so."

She frowns deeper and it's such a weird look on Lovely that I burst out laughing. She rolls her eyes before patting me on the back, making her way to her little cabin. I blow out a breath and make my way into the farmhouse. There's not much going on and I guess I should take some time to process what the hell happened.

Making my way onto the porch I'm not at all surprised when Tank steps out of the house. "Come on brother, you look like you need a seat and some quiet."

Throwing him a chin lift I follow him around the wraparound veranda, only stopping when we come to a comfy as hell looking swing chair. I stare at it a moment before raising a brow. We are both big fuckers, Tank only marginally smaller than me in width and height.

Tank throws back his head, a loud guffaw shaking his body, "Shit, nah we ain't both fitting on there. You sit, I'll lean," He flicks his head to the railing, crossing his arms and leaning back, one foot crossed in front of the other. "Wanna talk about it?"

"Not really, brother."

He nods thoughtfully, stroking his blonde stubble. "OK. wanna process it? Are you pissed she never told you? Sad you didn't know? Scared shitless?"

I snort, "All of the above except pissed."

His brows raise as he mulls over my words. Tank is a lot like me, tends to have a daily word limit. It's probably why we work so well together. We've been working Devil's Big Tow for at least six years now and I can't think of anywhere else or any other brother I'd like to work with.

He stands quietly, waiting for me to elaborate, but it's hard to explain. Seeing the twins - fuck, twins! Seeing them standing there, it was like I knew them. I recognised them but I couldn't quite put my finger on where I had met them. There was just this niggly feeling at the back of my brain, that I *knew* these kids. Once I found out why they seemed so familiar, it was like my body was struck by lightning. Their eyes, the boy's size, the girl's light brown hair. All of those things echoed my parents or myself. All somehow mixed perfectly with Kaia. The slope of their noses, the tilt of their chin. It was like a punch to the gut, but there was no anger or resentment. Just...hurt. Disappointment. A pit in my stomach, probably exactly the same that Kaia felt that day. Shit, if that's what she wanted to tell me, that she was pregnant when she found me with my jock friends and Chelsea, fuck. I can see why she would up and leave sticks. I would too. Pregnant to a guy that would get a blow job from another girl and then not defend her when the cool kids called her names? Even though we weren't exclusive or even dating, we were best friends. We lost our virginity to each other. And then some. We knew each other better than we knew ourselves. I knew she had trouble fitting in and instead of looking out for her, I let her walk away, alone.

I run a hand down my face, growling to myself. "I know I should be pissed, and maybe one day soon I will be. But at this point? I fucked up and so did she. But now we have the cartel breathing down our necks and I have two kids I need to get to know. It's a shit storm."

"So you claiming them?"

"The kids? Fuck yes."

"And Kaia?"

I give him a bored look. "If I did that she'd have my balls."

Tank snorts, straightens, and slaps me on the shoulder. "Let the games begin, brother." He starts to head away, leaving me to my thoughts, before spinning on his heel. "You need anything, an ice breaker to help get to know the kids, someone to run interference for you, shout out." He smiles, then it turns into a grin. "I'll send Mira."

I throw my head back and laugh, feeling better than I did a few moments ago. It's not ideal timing, but shit! When would it ever be ideal to find out you fathered kids fourteen years ago and never knew about it?

Thinking back over the years, I can't help but wonder if what Kaia did, in keeping it secret, was the best thing for both of us? I wouldn't have been a good husband or father back then. My mind was set on becoming a marine. Hell, I shipped out a month after Kaia left town. I would have had to even if I did find out she was pregnant. Squeezing my eyes shut I realize that even in that scenario she would have been left to shoulder the burden alone.

"Yo Judge! Your fam is here!" Rider's voice yells out. I'm

thankful he's not giving me any shit, but I can't imagine he'll hold off long.

Standing, I let out a breath. Kaia and the kids are a part of me, whether Kaia wants to be or not, so they're my responsibility to get settled and to keep them safe. I watch as they exit their crappy, older model Toyota hatchback, wondering how the hell my son managed to even fit in the back. The trunk is packed full of clothes and who knows what else. They stand in a line outside the vehicle, the boy slightly in front of his mom and sister. My heart swells a little watching him being so protective. He'll grow up to be a good man. Shit, he's almost a man now. Close to the same age Niko was when he turned up at the DRMC.

I make my way over to them, holding Kaia's gaze as it burns into mine.

"Thank you for coming."

"We didn't really have a choice," she grits out.

I nod in agreement. "No, I don't suppose you did. Ah, this is you over here," I gesture to them to follow me to where they'll be staying. "You're in this trailer. It's all new, Mama Debs, who is kind of like the MC Mom, she put fresh bedding on the beds and has stocked the pantry although we tend to share meals in the dining room." I rub my hand down my shaved bald head, the stubble itching my hand in a way that soothes me. Almost.

"Um thanks, that's, ah, nice of her," Kaia stammers, looking around the trailer.

It's two bedrooms, so the kids will have to share, but I'm sure after sharing a womb they should be OK for the short amount of time we'll be locked down. Hopefully.

"If you settle in I'll go get your things." I rush out, trying to make myself useful.

Before I reach the car I realize I'm being followed by two

shadows. Turning, I swallow when I take in their intense gazes. They get that from their mother.

"Um, hi." I cringe inside. I'm an ex-marine hardass fucking biker and that's all I could squeak out in front of two teenagers?

The girl grins, possibly smelling my fear. She bounces on her toes a little before opening her mouth. "Hi! I'm Annie-Bella, and you're my dad. Whoa." She takes a deep breath and then whispers, almost to herself, "I look kinda like you," she looks up at me with wonder in her eyes and I know she must be feeling the same thing as me. She's right. She does kinda look like me, but stunningly beautiful. Again I get a pit in my stomach and my chest squeezes painfully.

My attention snaps to her brother as he steps in front of her, shielding her from my gaze. "Quit it! He's not our dad," he says to his sister over his shoulder. She pouts, shoulders slumping slightly. He turns back to me, green eyes blazing, "Stay away from our mom. She told us about you, you know. It's all good that you'd rather hang with skanks than listen to what our mom had to say back then, but you can't just come in and take over. We're only here so we don't get killed by some douche canoes who have it in for you."

I have no idea what to say, so instead I swallow thickly, then nod. Picking up all the bags in their trunk in both hands, I quietly walk past the kids, ignoring Annie-Bella's whispers about how strong I am, and the boy's continued efforts to quell his sister's enthusiasm. Placing the bags just inside the door, Kaia spins around, pulled from her thoughts by my entrance.

"That's all of it," I mumble, trying hard not to stare.

She's even more beautiful than she was when we were young. Her brown skin glistens in the sunlight coming through the window, her oversized tee knotted at the back, showing off her plump ass in her yoga pants.

"Thank you."

"Um, can I ask you something?" she lets out a sigh, but she doesn't argue, so I take the chance. "Annie-Bella introduced herself. You named her after our mothers?"

A sad smile plays on her lush lips, "Yeah. After my mom died yours stepped in and taught me all the things a girl should know. Seemed wrong to only name Annie-Bella after mine."

I can feel the thickness in the back of my throat, the ache in my heart that even in the moment when she may have hated me, she never hated my family or what they meant to her.

Swallowing the emotion, I clear my throat, "And the boy? What did you name him?"

Her back stiffens, her gaze on a fixed point outside the kitchen window. "Jackson. Jackson James Kennedy."

My heart feels too big for my chest and my knees are weak. She named our son after me. Maybe not my first name, but my son bears my surname as his first.

"Thank you," I barely whisper out, before knocking twice on the door jamb and leaving.

I'll walk away today, let them get settled in, but it's the last time I'll ever walk away from them.

Kaia

Shit. I take a deep breath, before blowing away the memory of the hurt look on Leo's face. He has no reason to be hurt. Leo - dammit, Judge, is the one who decided he didn't want us. I need to remember that. He's Judge now. He isn't my Leo anymore.

He hasn't been since the day my last email went unanswered. One day I'll ask him about that, but it's not going to be today.

"You OK, Mom?" Jax's voice sounds uncertain.

I smile at my sweet boy, always quick to defend me and yet no clue how to deal with an emotional woman. He's been the man of the house for far longer than he ever should have been. Even when I tried to treat him like a little boy, he would still tell me "Momma, Poppa said that I have to be the man of the house, and look after you and Annie." Damn my father trying to teach my son how to be a man. Most of all, damn the bastard who took him away from us.

"I'm all good. We're here now and Judge was nice enough to let us stay." I give them both a tight smile.

"He seems nice," Annie-Bella says softly.

I let out a sigh. Annie has spent her life looking for a father figure. She thought she had it once. Hell, I thought she did too, and then he turned out to be the worst mistake of my life. At least from what I know of the DRMC they are good men. They'd never hurt women and children, so I guess Judge isn't too different from how he was when we were young.

"I think he is probably a good man. I don't think the DRMC has bad men in their club," I answer cautiously.

"I looked into them before we came here. They've done lots of stuff to stop trafficking of drugs and women and children, so the guy might be a giant dick, but he's probably a good guy. Even if he is a deadbeat dad," Jax adds. I don't even have the energy to correct his language. I'm all twisted up and have the beginnings of a headache thanks to having to shut down my business and cram our worldly goods in the back of my junker car in under an hour.

"Do you think he might want to get to know us?" my sweet

19

girl asks. She may be fourteen, but she's never had attitude or a mean bone in her body. Her brother got all that.

"That's something you have to ask him, baby girl. But just be mindful that the men have shit going down so they may not have time to be chatting to us," I reply, not wanting to build her hopes up.

I took his silence for all those years to mean that he didn't want to be a father. Seems odd that he'd be acting all twisted up about it now. But men are fucked up so who knows?

"Knock knock!" a cheery voice calls from outside before the door bursts open and we're greeted with a small, brown lady with short dark curly hair and a warm smile. "Kia ora! I'm Debs, but you can call me Mama Debs. I look after all these boys here."

"Don't you mean men?" Annie-Bella asks with a grin, obviously drawn in by this woman's motherly warmth.

"Psshh, no, they're boys. When you've seen them fight over the last brownie or whine over who smells the worst, they are definitely boys." She cups Annie-Bella's face, smiling gently at her before shifting her gaze to Jax. "Well, look at you two. A perfect blend between your mama and your papa, huh? Anyway, I came by to see if you want a tour? It'll be a quick one, but it'll give me a chance to introduce you to a lot of the people you'll be seeing around here. All of them come with their quirks, but they're good folk. Just like you." She smiles at us before circling her finger in the air, "Let's go!"

We follow the small whirlwind out of the trailer and along the path to a large farmhouse that sits proudly on the property. There are bikes in a neat line, all parked up with the front wheel facing out, as if waiting for the men to jump on and speed out at any moment. The friendly woman, Mama Debs, bounces up the steps. We follow a little more sedately. Actually, that's a lie, I follow with feet that feel like lead.

"Where are you from? You have an accent," Annie-Bella chirps, bouncing next to Mama Debs.

"Oh, I'm from Aotearoa, New Zealand." Mama Debs smiles kindly at her.

Her answer pulls me out of my thoughts. "Wait, what? How did you end up with an MC?" I ask, intrigued. I know from high school geography that New Zealand is a world away from Rose Grove, Texas.

Mama Debs giggles, facing me with a wide grin. "Would you believe that I ended up here because my daughter works for the Russian Bratva, and while visiting her, I ended up falling for Sidney Tombs and now I'm his Ol Lady?" Her eyes twinkle as mine grow wider.

"*You're* Debs! Oh my gosh I should have realized, Pops talks about you all the time!"

A soft smile pulls her cheeks up, making her eyes squint. "That man is such a romantic,"

I try to cover my snort. I've seen that man cause havoc with the Girl Gang in my diner. Especially with that god awful man Vi used to date. I have to admit I laughed out loud when Chewy "accidentally" squirted lemon juice in the man's eye.

"OK, here we are!" Looking around I realize that we've chatted our way into the house and up the stairs. Mama Debs gestures at me to walk through, but the door is closed so I decide to make myself known.

"Knock, knock?" I call quietly.

Mama Debs rolls her eyes and shoves past, throwing the door open.

"*Kotiro*, I'm sure you all know Kaia, and these are her babies."

Jax snorts behind her and my head spins in his direction, my angry eyes lasering into the side of his face. He quickly wipes the grin from his lips and clears his throat. "Jackson and Annie-Bella." Mama Debs finishes the introductions without blinking an eye.

The women all wave from their places around the room which looks to be a nursery. There are what seems to be a lot of babies and toddlers asleep, the women all in bean bags or on the beds with their children.

"Ooohhh, come closer, we need alllll the goss," Mira says, clapping her hands. I know her as the cheerleader of the group. Whenever they come into the diner she is always so positive about everything. I thought she was the normal one, perhaps not.

"Ae, good idea!" Mama Debs shoves me in their direction, "I'm going to take the kids to find Sage and Niko. They don't want to hang out with the mums and the babies." Debs bustles off as fast as she arrived and we all stare at her and my kids' retreating backs.

I could feel put out about the whole thing, or I can use this as a learning experience. "OK ladies, I need the full breakdown of what the hell is going on."

Chapter 3

Judge

"Is there a reason you're just creeping around?" I startle at the sound of Pops' voice close to my ear. So close I can feel his hot breath.

"I'm not creeping," I mumble, hoping he'll buy it.

"You are most definitely creeping. Trust me, I know a creep when I see one." I glare down at him only to be met with his stink eye. The same one Jules and his daughter sport.

"I'm just...looking."

"Riiiiiight."

I wait for him to leave, find another victim, but instead he stands next to me, watching Jackson and Annie-Bella chatting with Sage and Niko. I marvel at the size of Jackson. Knowing that he's only fourteen it's now obvious that his sister isn't little for her age, he's just large. He towers over Niko, who at twenty is no light weight himself.

"You know, you could, I don't know? Go and talk to them?" Pops doesn't look at me, just stands, hands in pockets without a care in the world.

I let out a sigh. It feels like that's all I've been doing today. "No, I can't. The boy, Jackson, hates me."

"Jax."

"What?"

"Jackson. He likes to be called 'Jax'."

I turn to stare at Pops. "How do you know that?"

"Oh, I don't know, I stopped 'looking' at them and asked? Jesus kid, are you simple or something?" Pops gives me a disgusted look, shaking his head.

I curse internally but don't make any move to do anything other than stare at the twins. Like a creep. Like Pops said.

"Can I give you some advice?" I nod. Pops' advice can't be any worse than what I'm doing, which is nothing.

"The only way to get to know them is to put yourself out there." He stares at me, holding my gaze before blowing out a breath. "You'll have to talk, Son. Use your words. Maybe tell them something about yourself and then ask them questions. That sort of shit. It ain't gonna be easy. Teenagers are notoriously hard to get to know, but you're patient so I bet you could win them over. If not, use your massive size to scare them into talking to you." He slaps me on the shoulder so hard he makes me sway a little. Jesus, he slaps hard.

Rubbing my shoulder I don't notice Annie-Bella sidling up to me.

"Hi," she says brightly, a grin on her face.

I'm shocked that she's here, let alone talking to me, so I stare wide-eyed at her for a beat too long, and her face starts to fall, taking my gut with it.

"No! Don't get upset, um, hi." I rub the back of my neck, "Sorry. I was just surprised you wanted to speak to me."

Her green eyes, so like mine and my mother's narrow, "Why?

24

Why wouldn't I want to speak to you? You're my Da-father, right? Unless you don't want to speak to me?" Her eyes dart away and I don't want her to think that. At all.

"No, I, ah, I'd love to talk to you. Do you want to maybe take a seat?" I gesture wildly around me, realizing that we're standing at the only part of the deck that doesn't have furniture.

"Sure!" She plops down on the ground at my feet, her legs dangling off the side of the deck.

She stares up at me, waiting. I gingerly lower myself down, knowing that it'll be hard getting my ass back up.

"Are you OK?" she asks, full of concern.

"Yeah. Just old," I huff.

"You're not *that* old," she rolls those familiar eyes. "You're the same age as Mom, maybe a couple of months older."

I raise my brows in surprise, side eyeing her. My daughter. "She told you that?"

"She told us everything." Annie-Bella shrugs. "Whatever questions we ask she gives us age appropriate answers. Once we hit thirteen she told us the whole thing. Probably to discourage us from making the same mistakes I guess. Not that she thinks we're a mistake," she rushes, "Probably more getting knocked up by you. I mean, seriously bruh, you were with another girl when Mom came to tell you the news? Not cool."

"Wow, she really did tell you everything," I mutter.

"Yeah, I guess she just wanted us to be able to have all the information to make well informed decisions."

My lips tilt up at that. Annie-Bella may look small and meek, but she's a firecracker. Just like her mom. We sit in silence for a moment, Jackson, I mean Jax, eyeing us warily.

"Is your brother OK with you being over here with me?"

Annie-Bella glares toward her brother before flipping the

25

bird and then doing the universal sign for jerking off. Then she puts on a sad face, balls her fists up and twists them in front of her face, miming crying, then the jerking sign again.

"He'll storm over here soon all full of piss and vinegar. He hates when I tease him about cracking." She grins up at me, showing off the dimples that my mom has.

"Cracking?" I frown down at her in confusion.

"Yeah, I overheard him playing with himself one day and I busted in on him to tell him to stop being gross and he started crying. Get it? Crying and jacking? Cracking? Oh, here he comes!" She bounces in place and I'm not sure what to do with that information. The way she blurted that out reminded me a little too much of Mira.

"What the hell has she told you?" Jax demands, placing his feet shoulder width apart, arms crossed over his chest. He would cut an intimidating figure to anyone who wasn't his sister I guess.

"Nothing. Just that your mom told you two everything," I answer, avoiding the whole cracking conversation.

"Well of course she did. How are we meant to make informed decisions if we don't have all the information?" His words mirror his sister's and I try not to smile at that.

"And, have you come to any kind of conclusion about me?" I hedge, wanting to know if I have a chance to get to know both of them, or only Annie-Bella.

They share a long look, and I swear it's like they have a full conversation without using words. They nod at each other before turning to me in unison. Almost creepily.

"We'd like you to want to get to know us, but we're stuck on the fact that you didn't want to know us before."

My brow furrows when I analyze Annie-Bella's words. "What

do you mean, before? I only found out about you this morning."

"Don't lie! Mom wrote to you! She emailed some lame address, Leoloveslasagne or some shit. You never replied to any of it!" Jax accuses, puffing up large and red with anger.

I raise my hands, trying to placate him. "Look kid, I know how this looks, but I can tell you now, I never got any emails. Shit, I totally forgot that email ever existed."

Looking between the two of them I can see Annie-Bella looking hopeful, but Jax is the harder sell. I'm not sure what I can do to convince them that I didn't know of their existence until I walked into the diner today.

Jax crosses his arms and shifts his weight to one foot, the other tapping the dusty ground impatiently. "Prove it. Pull up that email inbox and show me that none of my mom's emails were opened." He tips his chin at me, as if giving me the hurry up.

I nod mutely, pulling my phone from my pocket, my big fingers clumsy as I try to use the search app.

A giggle to my left has my gaze meeting Annie-Bella's, "Do you want me to do it? Your fingers are too huge. And you're old so you're probably not used to the tech." She holds her hand out and I place my phone in her small upturned palm. "Which email provider are you with?"

"Hotmail."

Jax snorts and I'm sure I hear him mutter "Boomer" under his breath. It doesn't piss me off like it did earlier. Huh. Maybe that's what happens when you have kids. They get less annoying.

"Leoloveslasagne, right?"

"Yeah," I clear my throat. In my defense, I was these kids' age when I made that up.

27

"Password?"

"Hopefully it's the same password I use for all that shit, LeoKaia91."

Both kids snort at that, obviously telepathically laughing about how old and lame I am, and then Annie-Bella gasps, turning the screen to her brother, her hand shaking.

"Oh shit," Jax whispers, staring wide at me.

"Here, Judge," Annie-Bella gently presses my phone into my hand. "Sorry," she whispers, giving me a small smile before she and Jax quietly leave me sitting on my ass. Alone.

Staring down at the phone in my hand, the small screen is lit up with a shit ton of unread emails, all from Kaia. Fuck.

Kaia

"So, let me get this straight, at one time or another, you have all been kidnapped?" I stare, wide eyed at the women who seem to be very relaxed about the whole thing.

"Well, kinda," Blanche tips her head from side to side. "Chewy and I got kidnapped on purpose."

"Aside from that one time the other two times I've just gone off on my own." Chewy adds.

"I was kidnapped," Vi raises her hand, the other on the sleeping back of her daughter.

"And fought like a hellcat," Ana beams at her. "I wasn't kidnapped, more held hostage for a moment."

"Oh, I was kidnapped by a human trafficking ring. That's how I met Chewy," Nat adds, her daughter wide awake on her lap.

28

"I was kidnapped, but I rescued myself so I don't think it counts," Remy's soft voice adds.

"I wasn't kidnapped, I lured them in. Reverse kidnap if you will," Pops' voice adds from the recliner he's sitting in, head back, eyes closed.

"I have never been snatched and now I'm feeling a little left out," Mira pouts.

"You've been the only one of us to have body parts sent as gifts, so there's that," Lovely adds, getting a huge smile in return.

"So, not *all* of us have been taken, but we've had shit go down,'" Chewy rounds out helpfully. "And now so have you! You're here because some cartel douche lord carved yours and your kids names into bullets. Welcome to the club!" She waves her hands around and smiles widely all while avoiding my gaze.

"No offense, but I'd rather not be part of the club, thanks."

"Too late! You're in! Besides, what else have you got going on? Just the diner probably, which I guess keeps you very busy and all, but here, being locked down with us, well you can make some new friends and maybe you can spend enough time with Judge to stop using your eyes to try to burn him to the ground," Mira shrugs.

I stare at her for a moment, before letting my gaze move to all the women. She just verbally vomited a lot of words at me, and some of them hit their mark. I've got nothing in my life outside of my kids and the diner. I've never really been popular or I guess friendly enough to have a lot of people around me. When I gave birth it was me and my dad at the hospital. No friends, nothing. Even before that, Leo was my only real friend. Like me, he was never really all that outgoing or popular when we were young. It's probably why we got on so well. That and his size meant that no one would ever pick on me. I knew I was the odd kid out at school. I had no mom. My dad did his best but he never really knew what a teenage girl would need. My clothes were never in fashion and add to that I had braces and a mop of hair from my black mom, my dad never quite knew how to look after it properly once she died.

"I'd have to spend eternity with him to not want to turn him to dust with just my gaze," I answer drily.

Lovely looks at me with a thoughtful look, "I know you said that you walked away when he was getting that blowjob and the cool kids teased you, but did you ever try telling him about your pregnancy after that?"

"Of course I did!" I throw my hands up. "He had a right to know. I tried calling and texting and everything went straight to voice mail. I sent emails all throughout the pregnancy. The last message I sent was the day after the twins were born, leaving it open for him to contact us. He never did."

"Idiot," Pops mutters under his breath.

"Has he ever explained himself?"

"Nope. And I'll never let him. As far as I'm concerned he is just the sperm donor to my kids. It's one thing to blow me off for your new friends; it's another to know you have kids and to ignore them completely. He's not the man I knew growing up. That's for sure."

"There has to be a reason? That doesn't sound like Judge," Mira says, brows furrowed.

"It doesn't, but men do dumb shit all the time." Vi waves her hand in the air.

"You'd know. You dated that idiot Josh for way too long," Remy points out then dodges the cushion thrown at her.

"Anyway, that's enough about me. What the hell are we going

to do about this cartel stuff? I have a house and a diner to get back to."

The women all eye each other for a moment, before nodding in unison. It's creepy, and something my twins do.

"We're going to take care of it," Chewy nods decisively.

"You mean, DRMC will take care of it?"

"Meh, something like that. I guess. If they don't, I will. So don't worry your pretty head." I eye Chewy for a moment, then remember that I've seen her in action.

"OK ladies, I've got to go find my other kids. If I leave them alone for too long, all hell breaks loose," Blanche announces.

"Her kids are kinda scary," Mira leans over and whispers out the side of her mouth to me.

"Wait, my kids are with her kids!" I frantically whisper back.

"How old are your kids?"

"They're fourteen."

Mira waves a hand at me. "Oh in that case, they're fine. They'll be with the older kids, Sage and Niko. They're like 19 and 20. It's the little ones you have to watch for."

I give her a nod, catching Lovely's eye. She smiles gently at me and gives me a thumbs up. The women all gather up their children if they're awake. If not Pops offers to keep an eye on them. How he can keep an eye on them through his closed eyelids, I have no clue.

Following them all out the door, and unsure what to do with myself, I loiter in the hall of the farmhouse, looking at the pictures on the wall.

"At a loss, *kotiro*? If so, you can give me a hand in the kitchen if you want." Mama Debs smiles at me, before disappearing to wherever she popped out from.

Following the sound of her singing, I find myself in a spacious, gorgeous home kitchen. Marble countertops, double ovens, a huge island and countertops around the perimeter. It's almost bigger than the diner kitchen, and a crap ton more luxurious.

"I know right?" she shoots me a knowing look. "Your twins were looking for you earlier. I told them you'll find them when you're ready. They're just out in the main room. I think they might be kicking Rider's ass."

"What!?"

"They're playing some video game," she grins at me, then turns to the pantry, removing things from the shelves.

I let out a snort at that. "Is, ah, Judge with them?"

She shoots me a tight smile, "No. He was a little out of sorts, I guess. He's up in his room,"

I nod, and my fists clench. The jerk. His kids are here and he still doesn't want to know them. Well, fine. I'll love them enough for the both of us. God knows I've been doing it all this time anyway. A warm hand lands on my shoulder, giving me a comforting squeeze. The contact shocks me, it's been a long time since anyone has touched me like this, out of care for me.

Mama Debs must see the shock on my face, because she tuts, "Aw, come here, baby girl." She pulls me into her deceptively strong arms, wrapping them around me and holding me. "It'll all work out."

"What will work out?" I whisper into her shoulder.

"Everything, you'll see."

Chapter 4

Judge

I work my way through the emails until I have one left. Some of them are burned into my brain and into my heart. The first two or three start off pissed. Then there's the ones that are resigned that I'll keep ignoring her forever. They seem to fluctuate between anger and sorrow and then there's the ones where she is struggling, and afraid.

"Leo,

I don't know if I can do this. There's two of them. Two people who will need me and I don't even remember my mom. How can I be a good mom when I don't have a role model? But that's not true, is it? I have your mom I guess. It's just scary to be doing this alone. I wish you were around to tell me it's going to be OK."

I blink the moisture out of my eyes. It's dated right when I left on my first deployment. I made it through boot camp and instead of going home I went straight to deployment. While Kaia was growing my babies I was in a sandbox in the middle of fucking nowhere, just as scared and as uncertain as she was. I roughly rub my eyes, blinking to clear them. If only I wasn't a dumb fuck. If only I had a thought in my head to even check these fucking messages. I'm all sorts of twisted up because there are so many mistakes that lead to me losing her and then not knowing I had kids out there. Sniffing, my finger hovers over the last unread email. Pressing it I wait for the window to open.

Leo,

I'm not too sure if you're getting these messages or if you're deleting them all, but I have to try. These are our babies. We have a boy and a girl. I know that I made the decision to have them, and I'm not asking you for anything.

I heard that you had joined the Marines and I know that you'll be good at it. You're probably too busy trying to stay alive to be worrying about some girl you went to school with.

Anyway, this is my current address or you can email me here if you want to see the twins. If I don't hear from you, then I guess this will be my last email.

Goodbye Leo, stay safe.

Scrolling down just a little a picture materializes, of two, tiny babies, one with a green hat, and one with a purple hat. I've never seen anything so fucking tiny in all my life, scrawny legs and arms, scrunched little faces. Most new babies I've seen look like potatoes or screwed up fists, but the twins steal my breath away with their beauty.

"Godammit Kaia!" I growl to myself.

My gut is screwed up and my chest aches at the thought that the only thing that kept me away was shame. Shame at the hurt I put on her face that day. Shame that I chose to get my rocks off with someone who was used by all the boys. Then I left it too long to apologize and the only choice I had was to run away overseas and fight other people's battles all because

I drove away my best friend with my shit decisions. Now what will keep me away is the shame that I could have been there all along. I could have supported Kaia through all her fears and pain. I could have held my babies when they were tiny, helped when they were sick or hurt, been there for all their firsts and yet I was fucking around while Kaia was busting her ass to give them the world.

Growling, I scrub my hand down my face. What a fucking waste of space. How the hell am I meant to look those kids in the eye and tell them that it was my dumb ass that kept them from knowing me? Fuck!

"Yo!" Rider bangs on the door after bursting through it, "Shit, glad you weren't rummaging in your pants over that hot little piece out there," he throws his thumb over his shoulder and I launch off the bed, pinning him to the door with my forearm across his throat.

"The fuck you just say?"

His eyes sparkle and his grin grows wider and wider at my irritation. "Nothing brother, just came to tell you dinner is served." He pats my chest, then runs his down it. "Wow, you've really been working out, big guy." He winks and then laughs his ass off when I shove him to the ground in the hall.

"I'm not hungry." He opens his mouth and I don't hear the rest, the door slamming in his face.

There is no way I'm going down there and having to look in the faces of Kaia and the twins until I sort my shit out. There's no other option.

"Yo! Get your big ass up!" I jerk, eyes flying open as I try to figure out where the fuck I am and what time it is. "Get. Your. Ass. Up!" is growled again and I use my abs to help me sit bolt upright until I'm staring at Pops and Mad Dog. Shit.

"Look kid, I get you got the shock of a fucking lifetime, but we kinda need your services." I frown at Pops who looks irritated back.

"Son, you've been up here for over 24 hours. What the fuck have you been doing?" Mad Dog asks, in a slightly gentler tone.

"He was having a pity party, that's what he was doing. I don't know why. Maybe because he could have had his family with him this whole time, a woman that fucking loves him and two beautiful kids and instead he traded that all for a blow job." Pops shakes his head, not even bothering to look in my direction.

"That true?" Mad Dog asks, staring right at me, arms crossed over his barrel chest.

"Yeah, in a nutshell." I'm embarrassed as fuck.

"That's a dick move, kid. I'm not sure she'll ever give you the time of day, but she's a sensible woman seeing as she's moved her family here."

"And she's been cooking up a storm feeding the brothers," Pops adds, eyeing me. "Your kids have been looking for you. It seems that they want to get to know you, and imagine their hurt when they find out you'd rather skip dinner than sit with them."

"Fuck!" I feel sick with rage and disappointment at myself. Jesus. What the hell is wrong with me? "Why do I keep fucking up?" I ask myself.

"Cos you're an idiot. And I hate to break it to ya, but you ain't got time to dwell on that. We've got the sheriff that's been messing with us and it's show time at the Office. Meet ya there. Unless you want to let us down, too," Pops snarks before leaving the room.

"He can be really bitchy, when he wants to be," Mad Dog says, watching Pops retreating back.

"He has a soft spot for the women," I answer, getting up and shoving my phone in my pocket.

"We all do, son. So, what's your plan?" Mad Dog asks, following me down the stairs and out the door.

We walk in silence for a moment. I try not to look into Kaia's trailer on my way past, but it's hard not to. It's getting dark out and the lights from inside her place illuminate her and the kids as they sit at the dinette together, laughing over something. It's the perfect vignette for the family. The only thing missing is me.

Mad Dog's massive hand comes down on my shoulder, giving it a rough shake. "You'll get them back. If that's what you want."

"I don't think she'd ever have me back. But just being able to spend time with them is more than I deserve."

"Then, we have to make it so." Mad Dog shrugs, walking on in front of me. "Don't waste time. Son, you've already wasted enough."

Kaia

Well, I don't know what I was expecting after the kids told me that Judge never opened any of the emails I sent, but it sure as hell wasn't radio silence. I would have thought we could have spoken about it. Perhaps apologize to each other, I mean, I know I owe him one. If I had known that he never got the messages, then perhaps I wouldn't have banned him from my diner. I was convinced all this time that he was a deadbeat dad and maybe I was wrong. Or maybe I was right because since the big reveal that he's a father to a set of twins, and that he never got my messages, he's been hiding. He didn't turn up to dinner last night and not to breakfast or lunch today either. I would know, I've been helping Mama Debs in the kitchen.

I know we're only here until the cartel stuff has been sorted, but it's not as bad as I thought it would be. It's peaceful, safe for the kids to roam around, and spending time with Debs is healing my inner child. Baking with her is like baking with my Mom. I was only little when she died, and my dad never remarried. I'd help him with dinner and baking for the school bake sales, but it's not quite the same as doing it with a mother figure.

"Are you sure you don't need us to come?" Annie-Bella breaks me out of my thoughts.

Smiling at her concerned face, I move to drop a kiss to the top of her curly head. "No baby, it's a ladies night, remember? Besides, I trust you and Jax to make good food and movie choices. I won't be gone long."

"We'll be fine," Jax's eyes roll. "We're pretty much grown and I don't ever remember you going on a girls night. So go and enjoy it, Mom."

I drop a kiss on his sweaty, smelly teenage boy head before waving and pulling the door closed behind me.

When I confronted Lovely this morning about what I heard last night - the screams of someone in extreme pain -I thought she would gaslight me and tell me that I didn't see or hear a thing. I know that I've been thinking of these women as friends, but to find out I'd been left out of whatever they were doing to those bad men from the diner pissed me off a little. I've become used to being left out of things, and I never had a lot of friends, but for some reason, that really hurt. Not just because I wasn't invited, but because I really wanted to hurt somebody too. There is no way I want someone out there to be threatening my babies and I don't get to bring them pain over it.

Instead of waving off my concerns, Lovely told me exactly what happened and why I wasn't invited. As the newbie it was deemed best for me to sit that one out. I guess I could see the thinking behind it. I'm new here and they don't really know me. But instead of leaving it at that, Lovely decided to throw together a girls night and now here I am, walking to Lovely's cabin, with strawberries and chocolate brownies in hand.

"Kaia! Wait up!" Spinning I catch Blanche power walking my way, with her little girl strapped to her chest.

I slow to a stop and wait for her at the bottom of the steps.

"Heard you were sad you missed out on the show? Don't worry, there will be others." She wags her brows at me, and for some reason, the promise of future violence makes me feel a little better.

"Sounds good to me," I smile back, walking through the open door.

"Mama needs a drink!" Ana announces, and I can't help myself, I burst into laughter.

We bustle around in the kitchen dining area before migrating to the couches, joined by Pops, Mad Dog and two Russian men Ana says are her best friend and his brother. I still have no clue how the hell a girl from small town New Zealand managed to befriend the Bratva, but it seems to work. She throws insults in Russian and teases Sasha about being the girl in his relationship with Roman. We all laugh at the big blonde man, and then I laugh even harder at the look on his brother's face.

"Soooo Kaia, how's everything going with Judge? Have you gotten the flutters of remembrance of the good times you shared with each other?" Mira waggles her eyebrows, "Oh oh! This would make the perfect second chance love story, I love a second chance. I've written a few of them, you know." She nods and I still marvel over the fact that she's a famous writer.

"OK, I admit, I love your second chance romance books, but there is no second chance for me and Judge. No way. There's too much water under the bridge, so to speak."

"I dunno girl, I think there's still a spark there," Pops adds, smirking.

"Nope! No way, nuh uh, you keep that smirk to yourself, Pops! I'm just here to keep my kids safe and then I can go home, back to the diner and continue to let Judge ignore us. I mean, I'm all for forgiving him, even if it was his fault that he never checked his damn emails."

"Boys are *so* dumb!" Ana slurs out.

"So dumb!" I agree. "But even after the fact, after the whole missed emails reveal, he still hasn't made any moves to get to know the kids or talk to me. The Leo I know would face things head on. Judge, well, he seems to be hiding his head in the sand. I don't need a man like that in my life."

Pops gives me a shrewd look, before nodding his head. "I'm just going to pop to the big house for some ice."

"So, you don't think you'd ever, in the history of the world, want to see Judge naked again?" Mira asks, a glint in her eye.

My core clenches and I have to tamp it down. When we were kids he was always handsome. Oh OK, I admit it, once we hit teen years he was the hottest thing on two legs. Thick, brown, wavy hair, bright green eyes, skin that tanned in the sun. He was always bigger than most of the kids our age, but with puberty came muscles. So many muscles. Now though? With that shaved bald head and tattoos and the scar just above his eyebrow? That shit can melt panties clean off your body.

"Nope," I lie through my teeth.

Nobody buys it either, they all laugh at my expense, even Dima who up until now has remained fairly stoic, sitting stiffly between his brother and Ana.

"If I had to hazard a guess, I'd say he would be good in the sack. He's all intense and stuff," Chewy says, looking thoughtful. "He wouldn't be as good as Rhodie though. He's perfect. And he lets me do things to him."

"For shit's sake Chewy, do not mention any more butt stuff with my kid!" Mad Dog grumbles.

"But he's just such a giving lover!" she argues back with a glint in her eye.

Lovely plops down next to me on the couch. "Pretty crazy, huh?" I smile, nodding in agreement. "Feels good though, right?"

Turning to her, her kind eyes hold my gaze, long enough to make me tear up.

"You're not alone anymore, Kaia. No matter what happens with you or Judge or the kids, you have us now."

"Thank you," I whisper.

"What she said!" Pops yells out, back from the big house drawing attention to us. "You're girl gang now, girl. So if Judge doesn't sort his shit out, I'll do it for him."

"We're always open to a little ass kicking," Mad Dog adds with a grin.

"Hey! Since we're here and we've got all night *and* we have new members-" Mira waves at me and then Sasha and Dima,

"I say we play a get to know you game."

Some of the women cheer and I look at Sasha and Dima on the couch in horror. No way. Not happening. There is nothing worse than getting up and sharing stuff about yourself. Judging by the groans from some of the other women, namely Remy and Blanche, I can tell they aren't down with the idea either.

"I dislike sharing with people," Chewy bluntly states.

"Says the woman who likes to talk about Rhodie's ass," Nat says under her breath, causing me to snort into my wine glass.

Mira's wide eyes narrow, "OK, well, how about this, we'll call it 'Would you ride it?' and we each come up with a character description, then the person whose turn it is has to answer if they'd ride it or not. I'll *definitely* be able to tell a lot about you from your answers," she waggles her brows and this seems less sweat-inducing than the alternative.

"Nat, you're the first victim. Ummm," her face screws up before she brightens, and I can just tell it'll be a doozy, "He's 6'5", voice that could melt your panties, rides a hog called Lucifer, but he says 'yum yum in my tum tum' everytime he eats vajayjay?"

We all stare at Mira in horror.

"Ew," Pops says, looking grossed the hell out. To be fair, we all are.

"Is it a one off ride, or a long term ride?" Mad Dog asks. Pops gives him the side eye, frowning, "What? It's good to know the rules," he grumbles under his breath.

"Oh, it can be as long a time as you like," Mira grins.

We turn to Nat, waiting with bated breath. Even Dima, who seems to have no expression at all, is leaning forward, waiting for her answer.

Nat takes a deep breath, "Ride. With ear plugs." She grins.

"Good work around," Remy says, the rest of us women nodding in agreement.

"Oh, I want to go next!" Ana waves her hand in the air. "Sasha, this one's for you," she has a glint in her eye as she stares at her best friend. "He looks like Jason Momoa, but he has an aggressively unkempt bush. That he refuses to manscape."

"Jesus," Lovely whispers and it makes me snort laugh because, I mean, it's Lovely. She shared a little about her background with me today, and she's told me she has faith, but doesn't really feel the same way about religion as she once did. So for her to be using Jesus' name, well, shit.

"How aggressive are we talking?" All heads whip toward Mad Dog, and I can see the glint in Pops' eye as he moves to open his mouth. "It's for research purposes!" Mad Dog barks before Pops can even say anything.

"Yeah, what he said," Sasha agrees, waving in Mad Dog's direction.

"Thick, black, hard to locate the peen."

"Holy shit," one of the other women whisper. I'm not too sure which one, my eyes are on Sasha as he looks green around the gills.

"*Blyat*, hard pass you asshole."

Ana bursts into laughter, leaning over Dima to slap Sasha wherever she can reach. "Yeah OK, asshole," she replies.

"Oh, oh, I have one for Mad Dog!" Pops smirks in Mad Dog's direction. Mad Dog's eyes narrow and he nods at Pops, doing the "bring it on" motion with his hands. "Beautiful, stacked with all natural breasts, long legs, gorgeous figure. Super interested in you."

"But?" Mad Dog raises a brow.

"But she makes you wear a bell so you can't sneak up on people and she puts you on a diet for your diabetes."

"I don't have fucking diabetes!" Mad Dog roars, lunging for Pops who is up and darting away a lot damn quicker than a man of his age should.

"Is it always like this?" Dima asks me.

"I have no idea, I'm new," I shrug.

He holds my gaze for a beat too long, his brows furrowing briefly and his eyes narrowing. I swear they change color too, but that would be weird, right?

"You're safe while you're with people you trust," he murmurs, giving me a small smile.

"Uh, thanks," I return his smile, but the way he worded that sounded odd.

I roll his sentence over in my mind a little, and then decide to let it go. He has a thick accent and maybe he just got his words mixed up.

"Who wants to blow something up?" Chewy says abruptly.

We all look at each other in silence, before hands start shooting up all over the room.

"Now that's the kind of getting to know you we like!" Pops claps his hands, rubbing them together.

"Choice of weapon can tell you a lot about a person," Sasha agrees.

"Anyone got a rocket launcher?" I joke, to get the ball rolling.

"Ooohhh, a woman with taste! I like it!" Chewy says, grinning at me, her gaze flicking to mine briefly before dancing away.

"What does that tell you about me, Mad Dog?" I grin cheekily.

"It's dramatic as fuck. You're about as subtle as a sledge-hammer and aren't taking shit from no one. You're a super protective momma bear and given you picked a weapon that powerful with the ability to take down anyone in its path makes you a total wild card. You'll fit in well here, sweetheart."

Wiping moisture from my cheeks I feel a weight lift off me for the first time since my dad died. I finally feel like I fit and that's one hell of a feeling.

Chapter 5

Judge

Clenching my fist I bring it up to gently knock on Kaia's door. I feel like shit that I haven't turned up before now, but fear will do a lot to a man. Like send him into a spiralling depression, make him sleep for 24 hours straight and then give him the screaming shits from hell. As soon as my stomach felt like it could handle a confrontation, I came here. To Kaia and the kids' trailer. And then proceeded to stand out here for ten minutes.

"Whatcha doing?" Spinning I'm pinned to the spot by two sets of green eyes.

"Hey, I was looking for your mom,"

"She's on a girls night," Annie-Bella answers, walking up the steps, pushing open the door and walking past me.

"Oh, OK, I'll come back some other time." I turn to leave, only to be blocked by Jax, arms crossed, feet planted. Pretty much his standard I've noticed.

"What, don't want to spend time with us?" he asks, one brow raised.

"No, I'd ah, I'd love to, if that's OK with you and your sister?" He shrugs, moving to walk past me, much like his sister did. "It's up to us if we want to hang out with you. Just like it's up to Mom whether she wants to talk to you or just ignore you and the fourteen years of no contact."

Ouch. I guess I deserved that.

"Well, you coming in or not?"

I hurry in behind him, shutting the door and then realizing that this trailer is probably not built for two, large people to be inside it. Annie-Bella must notice too because she giggles, then spins to pull an extra plate out of the cupboard.

"Wait, if your mom is at girls night," which scares me to my very core, "What were you two doing before you caught me?"

"We'd gone to pick up the dinner Mama Debs made us. It's kinda like lockdown takeout, don't you think?" Annie-Bella grins.

"Just don't eat too much, she only made enough for us. We'll share, but go easy." Jax eyes me for a moment. "You look like you eat a lot."

"I guess from that statement, you do too," I nod toward him and I'm sure I see him puff up a little, proud that I'd noticed his physique.

"Stop being a dick," Annie-Bella chides her brother, "a blind man could see that you eat all the food." She waves a hand in his direction before turning to me. "It's why I'm so small, Jax took all the in utero nutrients."

"Hate to break it to you sweetheart, but I think you're small because your mom is tiny." My daughter beams at the endearment, and I realize how much having me around means to her. To them both, maybe.

"What was she like when you were younger?" Annie asks,

and I don't miss when her brother moves closer, wanting to hear my answer.

"Well, we met in kindergarten and she was so small. The smallest kid in class for almost all the years. She couldn't get herself going on the swing because she was so tiny, so I pushed her on it and then we kinda never were apart after that. Probably helped we lived on the same street and our parents were friends." They're both wide-eyed, and I guess I understand. To them she's just their mom. The woman who has selflessly looked out for them all this time. It's probably crazy for them to think she was once a child.

"Why did you do it?" Jax asks, knowing I'd pick up the context.

"We weren't cool kids, your mom and I. I guess, shit, I don't really know. One minute I was a dweeb, the next I was on the football team and I had all these friends."

"They weren't really friends," Annie whispers, and I shake my head in agreement.

"I was dumb and then Kaia, she was just...gone. I was heartbroken. Not as much as she was," I add quickly as I could see Jax about to refute that.

"And now?"

"Now I'm heartbroken for a completely different reason. If you are open to it, I'd love to spend some time with you both."

They do that thing where they share a look, then turn back to me. "How do you feel about Die Hard?"

I sit stiffly on the recliner, my size not conducive to being stuffed into this tiny chair. The kids are sprawled out on the larger couch and I don't miss their eyes darting toward me and their snickers. I feel put on the spot and I hate that feeling.

"Are you hot?" Annie's voice breaks through my haze, the

sound of John McLaine's gunshots on the big screen jolting me.

"No, I'm feeling pretty comfortable. Are you hot? Do you need me to open a window?" I jump up, wanting to do anything to make her feel at ease.

"No, I'm fine, it's just, um, your head is really shiny. Like *really* shiny. And you look sweaty." She gives me a tight smile. "Just wanted to make sure you're OK. Sage is busy with the big little kids at the moment, and I'd hate for you to have a heart attack and die."

I stare at two sets of eyes, identical to mine, although where Annie-Bella's are wide with concern, Jax's look as thought he's going to fucking breakdown and piss himself at any moment.

"No, sweetheart, I'm good."

"OK," she replies happily before glancing at me again. "So, is male pattern baldness on your side of the family or is it a choice? Because you know Turkey does some pretty cool hair transplants. You'd have to walk around in a sweat band for a while and your head swells up like a beach ball, so it may not be that cool."

Jax loses his fight and snorts so hard he chokes on it. Little shit.

"Ah, it's a choice." I answer, hoping that if I stare at the TV the interrogation will come to an end.

"Hm. Interesting choice," is all she says.

What the hell? I thought that fucker, what was his name? Rodney? I thought he was a one off with his observations and shit talk. Turns out, my kids are the same, although it's delivered in a very sweet, very cute package. We settle in again, the kids only eyeing me every now and then until we're sitting in relative companionship watching people get blown to smithereens. A large boom from outside the trailer has us all jumping up, before I take the kids to the floor, my bulk covering them. My heart is racing and I growl at the kids to stay down until I say.

Another small explosion rocks the place and I move my hand along my leg, flicking the holster at my ankle, freezing when I hear cackling and yahooing.

Rolling off the kids, I check to make sure they're alright. "It's OK. It's just girls night."

"What the actual fuck!?" My brows raise at Jax's language. "What the hell are they doing to make that noise?"

"Chewy has a rocket launcher."

"Oh sick!" the kids say in unison, rushing to look out the window.

"Yeah, so sick," I mutter. Great. One evening and Chewy is already cooler than me. Shit, am I a lame dad? Looking down at my feet I wonder if I need to buy some dad sneakers.

"Do you think-"

"Nope, your mother would kill you and then probably me for telling you. Just go sit your ass on the couch, I want to see the end." My eyes widen when I realize I may have completely overstepped.

"You're getting the hang of this dad thing," Annie-Bella says with a grin, walking to the couch and flopping down, her brother following suit.

"While you're up, grab the brownies, old man," Jax calls out, and I really want to dump the brownies on his goofy fucking hair cut, but I contain myself. He's my kid and I love him. Even though he has jerk tendencies. But I guess it is what it is. The kid is trying to push my buttons, testing me. Well, he better buckle up, because I won't lose.

Delivering the brownies *nicely* I retake my seat, and settle in again.

* * *

I'm jolted awake by the sound of rummaging and banging in the doorway, a shooting pain running through my neck when I turn too fast. "Shit!" is hissed out and then comes a giggle. I know that sound.

"Kaia?"

"What the fuck?"

Standing from where I've slumped in the recliner, my breath catches at the sight of her. Hair a mess around her shoulders, eyes bright, cheeks flushed.

"What the shit are you doing here? Have you been stalking me?" Her eyes narrow dangerously and I'm not sure if she can even see me clearly through them.

"Shit no! I came earlier looking for you, instead the twins invited me in and we had dinner and watched a movie." Looking around at the deserted living area, I must have fallen asleep and they ditched me.

"Oh," she stands there, staring. "I got to shoot a rocket launcher. I blew shit up!" She mimes an explosion, giggles and then stares at me some more.

"I better get going, leave you to it." I pat my pockets, making sure I have my phone and whatever other shit I might possibly need, before moving toward the door.

"Thank you," she whispers.

"What for?"

"For seeing them. Thank you."

51

I nod once, wanting to say so much fucking more, but it's stuck in my throat. Besides, she may not want to listen to me today. Or even maybe tomorrow. Pulling the door closed behind me I stumble when my shirt is grabbed and I'm dragged from the step.

"What the fuck!?"

"Listen here numbnuts, I have a plan. You want that family to be yours right?" Pops' voice hisses at me and I should have known he'd be the only bastard here brave enough to jump me late at night.

"What the hell man!?"

"Answer me!"

"Yes! I want them to be mine. Even Kaia, if she'll have me." Wow. Looks like the words I wanted to say to Kaia that were stuck just come flying out when my defenses are down.

"Good. Tomorrow you're going to ask her on a date."

I stare at Pops in the darkness, the only light coming from the main room in the farmhouse. "Come again?"

"Ask. Her. On. A. Date." He emphasises each word by shaking me around by the scruff of my shirt.

I let out a breath. "Look, dude. You know we're on lockdown. I can't take her anywhere."

"I know that, that's why we're bringing the date to you. Do you trust me?"

I think about it for a split second. I don't *not* trust him. But at the same time the guy does have a tendency to get into trouble.

"Come on kid, it's an easy question."

Making up my mind, I blow out a breath. "Yes, I trust you."

"Good. Let the Love Pres take care of everything."

My brows shoot up to my non-existent hairline. "The Love Pres?"

"Some people call me that."

"Who?"

"Your Pres for one."

That sounds pretty fucking unlikely but I decide to let it go. I mean, shit, Pops knows more about Kaia and the kids than anyone here. He's a trusted member of the girl gang. He'll know more about what Kaia is thinking and feeling than anyone else here.

"OK, Love Pres. What do I have to do?"

Kaia

Banging on the door has me rushing to answer it. I know that the men are meant to be riding out tomorrow, but what I've learned from the women over the course of our girls night drinks is that shit can hit the fan quicker than the blink of an eye.

Flinging the door open I'm met with Pops, and he looks like he means business.

"Listen, girl, I like you. You're one of us. But for the love of god, I need you to say yes to the next person that knocks on this door, capiche?"

I blink once, then twice. "What? Who's going to knock? What's the question?"

"You don't need to worry about that, just say yes." With that his hand snakes inside, grips the door handle and then slams the door in my face. "Maybe put on some lipstick!"

What the hell? I look at my distorted reflection in the microwave and then jump out of my skin when someone bangs on the door.

"What the hell, Pops!" I yell as I fling the door open again, only to jolt and let out a squeak when I'm met with Judge's large body blocking out the sunlight.

"Kaia," he breathes out, staring like he hasn't seen me in years. I guess it's not too far from the truth. Apart from last night we haven't really been in each other's vicinity long enough for a full conversation. I've spent more time with his brothers.

"Judge." I ignore the flinch when I call him by his road name, and not his real name. Yes, I know all about road names now. Still have no idea how the guys got them, just that the only people to call them by their government names are their Ol Ladies.

"I was wondering if you would like to join me for dinner tonight?" He looks nervous as hell. So I make him sweat, for the laughs.

He rocks from foot to foot, first staring too intently at me, and then looking at something over my shoulder. I stare him down, knowing that he's hella uncomfortable. Then I remember Pops' words and I guess it'd be a good time to finally have a reason to talk.

"OK."

His eyes flick to me in surprise, "OK?"

"Yeah. Yes. OK, I'll have dinner with you."

"I'll pick you up at 6pm."

He turns to walk off. "Wait, we're on lockdown, wouldn't we just be eating here?"

He turns toward me and damn the sunlight beaming down on him. It's giving him a hazy look, like he's been lit up by damn angels or something. It's also highlighting how incredibly handsome he is. This is something I don't need. There is no need for me to look at this man as anything other than the guy I grew up with. *And had hot, soul shattering sex with. Two times.* I shake my head, to dispel the thoughts and concentrate on the not hot man staring at me.

"Pops has got everything arranged." He shrugs one broad shoulder.

"Well, OK then. See you at 6." He smiles that lopsided smile I used to love before walking away with a bounce in his step.

I watch his ass work behind the fabric of his jeans and wonder if I should maybe ask for his glute workout regime and then remember that that ass has been a total ass this whole time and to not be a weak willed woman. I've been in trouble before thanks to pretty looks and hard thighs and I don't need that kind of trouble in my life again. For shit's sake, I'm hiding out from the cartel as we speak.

"I saw what you were looking at," a droll voice calls out.

I flip the bird in Rider's direction and ignore his laughter as I shut the door behind me. I have hours to go before Judge collects me, and in the meantime there are things I want to try making in the farmhouse kitchen. My aunt's jambalaya will go down a treat and can just simmer away until it's ready to be eaten.

Gathering up the spices that I refuse to go anywhere without, I make my way to the farmhouse kitchen, nodding at Sniper along the way. I'm not sure of the man's story, but something definitely haunts him.

"Hey, little lady, need a hand with anything?" Mad Dog calls out, already making his way down the front steps of the house toward me.

Before I can reply he has my little basket of spices out of my hands and into his much larger ones.

"Oh, are you cooking?" another voice nearby calls.

Swinging my head around I'm met with Nitro pushing Fox in a wheelchair along the deck. I roll my eyes, grin and continue making my way into the kitchen. The kitchen that thankfully is large and roomy, because somewhere along the way I've picked up more giant bikers all clamouring to see what I'm up to.

Spinning, I place my hands on my hips and stare them down. "I never see you all in here crowding around Mama Debs when she's cooking."

"That's because we know we're gonna get the good stuff." My brow raises at Rider whose face turns pale before he starts backtracking, "I mean, we know you'll give us the good stuff too, because the diner and all that, but we don't know your repertoire yet."

"Good save," Switch tries to whisper but instead it reverberates off the walls.

"What he's trying to say, but can't because he's a dumbass, is that you have a whole new set of meals that we would love to try, if it's OK with you," Fox smiles sweetly. Nitro presses a kiss to the top of his head, his hand resting on his shoulder.

They are the sweetest couple, but I was shocked to find out that this is a new development, brought on by the clubhouse attack. Watching them for a moment I can't help but think that as shocking and awful as the attack was, some good came out of it.

I'm pulled from my thoughts by Rider, which is probably a good thing because I think I was staring like a creep at Fox and Nitro. "So, whatcha making?"

"Jambalaya. And all y'all gonna help me. Wash your hands, stand in a line, and I'll give you your orders." I clap my hands twice and they all rush to the sink.

A warm, heavy arm is slung over my shoulder, and I lean a little closer. I knew it was Pops straight away from his spicy cologne. "I heard you were making jambalaya. Gonna be spicy, right?"

My brow raises. I don't know how it happened so fast, but I feel like I can trust this man with my life. But at the same time, I feel like I can't trust him at all. He has a glint in his eye and I'm not sure if it's going to come back on me, or hit the MC with full force.

"Sure, I mean, I can make a good spicy batch for the adults and a more mild batch for the kids."

"I knew I liked you for a reason. I'm gonna wash up and help out." He flicks me a wink and I side eye him as he walks toward the sink. Shrugging, I make my way around the kitchen, inspecting the clean hands and handing out jobs.

"Ah, shit, this pepper is making me cry," Rider sniffs, rubbing his eyes with the heel of his hand.

"What pepper?" Screaming ensues and I rush toward Rider, but the sound isn't coming from him. "Dex? Shit, are you OK?"

His face is red and tears are streaming down his face, pants around his ankles.

"What the fuuu-" Mad Dog stares, speechless

"My balls are on fire!"

Chaos breaks out, with half the men falling to the ground pissing themselves laughing, while the others stare at Dex's very red looking privates in horror.

"Here!"

A splash and then a glugging sound fills the air as I stare at

Rhodie holding an upended three gallon jug of milk over Dex's head.

"Not my face, my junk!" Dex yells shrilly.

"Ew! You wash your own cock off," Rhodie says, shoving the milk jug into Dex's chest.

Milk runs down Dex's firm stomach, pouring directly onto his junk, his groans of relief causing my cheeks to heat.

"*Aue!* What the hell is going on in here? Dex! This is a kitchen, put your *raho* away!" Mama Debs chides, flapping her dish towel at the men, whipping their butts to get them to move out of the mess that Dex has made.

"It's not my fault! The pepper Pops gave me to cut must have got on my hands or something and then ended up on my cock and balls and it burns!" Dex whines.

He's so pitiful looking that I can't help but feel sorry for him. Then his words register. "Wait, what do you mean, the pepper Pops gave you?"

I slowly look around the room, trying to locate Pops and he's nowhere to be seen.

"That son of a bitch! He pepper pranked us!" Rider growls, his eyes still red and irritated from the pepper he was cutting.

"He was sabotaging my jambalaya! I knew he looked dodgy like he was up to something!" I exclaim, oh, he's going to pay for that!

"I think you'll find he was sabotaging us, not your delicious food," Nitro offers, but it still doesn't help me.

"Nope. Pops is going to pay the piper. You don't mess with a woman's jambalaya."

"Oohhh, what are we going to do?" Dex asks, his face looking a lot less red.

"What do you mean, we?"

"He pranked us, and you. If you have plans, girl, you gotta let us in."

"Oh I'll have a plan. I just need to do research first. He'll keep." I smile at the men, then my smile turns into a wide grin until I'm beaming.

"Ah shit, we got another loose cannon, brothers," Rider laments, shaking his head sadly.

That just makes me throw my head back and laugh.

"*Kotiro*, you have a date to get to. I'll take care of this, you go pretty yourself up," Mama Debs shoos.

"You better tell your man we're coming for him," I say cheerily on my way out.

"Oh, I'll join you. You don't mess with a woman's kitchen."

The men all stand on either side of the door, high fiving me on my way out. I don't think I've had this much fun in a long time. Now to face the father of my children.

Chapter 6

Judge

It shouldn't surprise me that the big littles have this badass hideout, but it does. When I was a kid my dad built me a clubhouse. It was only for me and Kaia, so it was basically a box. We furnished it with beanbags and had my old metal lunchbox that we kept snacks in. These kids have a room almost the size of our common room at the clubhouse, complete with a kitchenette, electricity and a TV on the wall.

"What is this place?" Kaia asks, head swivelling to take it all in.

"It's the big littles' hideout," I reply, taking in her beautiful face as she looks around the room.

The hideout is decorated with twinkly lights, soft music playing in the background and there are tables dotted around. Kaia and I are at one, Blanche and Tav at another. Pops and Mama Debs are across the room and Kaia keeps shooting daggers at Pops every now and then so he's avoiding all eye contact.

"What did Pops do to you?"

She brings her chocolate-colored gaze to mine, my heartbeat stuttering for a moment. "The brothers were helping me make jambalaya. He pranked them by switching out my peppers for some ghost peppers."

My lips twitch. Shit. She won't let this lie.

"Would you like anything to drink, sir, madam?" Turning to my left has me looking at Jax's narrowed eyes and fake smile. "You better behave," he murmurs. The kid would make a great ventriloquist.

"Jax!" His mother barks at him. "It's just dinner, jeez. And yes, I would love a wine, thank you." She gives him a sweet smile as he pours the liquid in her glass. "And is this where you and your sister have been all day?"

"Pops needed a hand and someone to keep the big littles in order," he replies, pushing a glass of water my way.

"How's that going for ya?" I ask, bringing my water glass to my lips. I'm not drinking tonight anyway. Not with our mission tomorrow.

"I think there's something wrong with these kids."

I snort and then choke on my water. I mean, he's not wrong. There is definitely something different about those kids. I'm not too sure if it's The Keep's genetics or Blanche's parenting. Although Jovie is just as bad and she's not a Keep kid.

He wanders off to somewhere behind a curtain. Whoever is back there seems to be at the mercy of Cove, barking instructions like a drill sergeant.

"So, um, I guess I wanted to say sorry for banning you from the diner. It seems unfair now, given you didn't know about the twins." Kaia's eyes are boring into mine, and the intensity is too much for me to bear. I move my gaze over her shoulder, and nod.

61

I sit in silence for a moment. Unsure what to say. It used to be so easy between us. I could share everything with Kaia, all my inner thoughts and feelings. I didn't need to wax lyrical or anything, but a short three word sentence on how I was feeling and she'd be able to read the rest. That was a lifetime ago and now she's here, staring at me like she wants me to say something. I have so many words, and yet none want to come out.

"It's OK," I muster up after too long a pause.

Darting my eyes to her face I'm met with a frown. She fiddles with her cutlery, looking around, preferring to watch the other couples than engage with someone so verbally backed up that I'll need a colonoscopy to get the words out.

I follow her gaze, to where it's lingering on Fox and Nitro. "It's new. Them, being together."

Her eyes flick to mine. "I heard. It's kinda sweet, best friends to lovers type thing." She huffs.

"Huh?"

She rolls those chocolatey eyes, and it sends me hurtling back through the years. "Mira could probably explain it better."

"She uses too many words."

Kaia snorts, taking a sip of her wine, her shoulders relaxing slightly. "Best friends to lovers is a romance book trope. It's pretty much what it says on the tin. Best friends fall in love with each other but neither wants to make the first move in case it ruins the friendship or whatever. Usually there's a catalyst to get them together. It might be one of them starts dating and the other gets jealous, or –"

"Or one of them gets shot?" I finish for her, eyes on my brothers.

"Yeah, something like that."

I wait a moment, working the words over in mind as Kaia takes another sip from her glass. "Kinda like us, almost." My eyes dart in her direction.

Her face falls slightly and it makes my chest tighten. I watch as she pulls herself back together, piece by piece until she looks unbothered by the conversation. I've seen her do this time and time again growing up, and yet somehow she never looked this alone, this fragile. I know it's not my place to ask what she's been through, not yet. I need to gain her friendship, her trust back before I can even think to ask such things.

She shakes her head, plastering a smile on her face, her eyes still holding shadows. "Not quite like us. We're more best friends to lovers to enemies. That's a thing, too."

I stare at her. "Seriously?"

She laughs and it strips the tension a little. "Seriously. Women have long been neglected in the book world. There's all sorts of tropes."

"Mira talks about them a lot, but I thought she was just making stuff up. I mean, half the time I'm not even sure I get the full sentence when she talks."

Kaia giggles, and the sound makes me want to make her laugh all the time. Forever.

"I love her. I love all the women. Did I tell you I got to fire a rocket launcher?"

I mirror her grin. "Yeah. The kids were pissed they never got to fire it."

She starts shaking her head back and forth before I even finish speaking. "Nope, nuh uh, no way! Those two can cause trouble without military grade weapons."

"I don't know, they seem pretty innocent to me," I joke.

A look crosses Kaia's face and I watch as those damn shadows take over again. I knew this woman like the back of my own god damned hand for most of my childhood. She's gone through some shit and come out the other side. I just know it.

"You're a fantastic mom, Kaia. I wouldn't trust anyone else in the world to raise my children."

She sniffs and looks over my shoulder, "You don't know what type of mother I'm like, Judge, and your confidence is misplaced. But thank you for using your words." She gives me a sad smile.

"Dinner is served!" Cove's shout right next to us makes Kaia jump but it's the jolt we needed as she throws her head back and laughs.

"Thanks, Cove," I grin as she walks away in her snazzy looking head chef outfit.

All the kids look great, the waiting staff - the big kids, including mine - are all dressed in smart black attire. Jovie seems to be holding down a few roles, both in the kitchen and outside. Elio is being himself, attempting to socialise but instead placing dinner plates of bolognese in front of Tav and Blanche with little to no interaction.

"Bolognese for the lady, and the gentleman," Annie-Bella grins, placing first her mother's and then my meal in front of us. "Enjoy!"

"Thank you, Belly," Kaia murmurs, pressing a kiss to Annie's temple.

My brows pinch and I gotta ask, "Did you just call her-"

Kaia giggles, swallowing her mouthful, "Yeah, sorry. Her name is just a mouthful sometimes, so I sometimes call her Belly. Have since she was little."

A smile breaks out across my face, it's damned cute.

"Jax calls her Fanny-Smella when she pisses him off."

I blink, once, twice before throwing my head back and roaring. "That's siblings for ya."

We grin at each other, and I enjoy the food and the company. I can't say that Kaia won't stab me in the balls when I least expect it, but at this very moment it feels like there's a short burst where the years between us disappear and I'm here, with my best friend.

"Thank you, Kaia, for agreeing to dinner."

"Thank you for asking, I guess. Although I have a feeling Pops had a lot to do with it." She grins in Pops' direction, catching his gaze enough to point at her eyes, then back at him in the universal sign for "I'm watching you". Pops' back stiffens and I stifle a laugh.

"Kaia, after all this shit is over and done with, would it be OK if I visited with the kids? Not too often, it'd be up to your discretion and all that, but I'd, um, I'd like to get to know them."

She stares at me, and I can see her brain working. I hold my breath, hoping like hell she agrees. "It'll be up to them to agree, but I don't have a problem with it. Just, just don't break their hearts, OK?" Her eyes implore me and I fucking know they've been hurt in the past. The urge to get to the bottom of this shit burns in my gut but I need to tread softly here.

"I promise, with everything in me that I'll protect them."

She nods once and the relief in her eyes guts me. She may have my word that I'll protect their hearts, but I'm hell bent on protecting hers too.

Kaia

Damn Judge and his ability to read me so well. I thought after fourteen years apart that I'd have learned to cover my tracks better, learned to lie better, or at the very least hide my emotions. But when it comes to the way I feel about my kids and what they've been through, its fucking hard to bury all those emotions and memories.

I knew from the look on his face at dinner that he knew something was up. We may have not seen each other in years, but all the signs were there. The set of his jaw, the way his eyes narrowed. He wanted to grill me until I told him what was wrong. It was always his way. No matter how many kids picked on me or called me names, no matter how hard I thought I had hid my hurt, he always knew. And then he'd interrogate me until I spilled my guts and he would fix it. Either with his fist or his scary glare. I mean, the guy was near six foot when we were eleven years old, he was also wide as hell, so all it would take is a look and the kids would back off. Leo was my protector, Judge is my co-parent. Someone who thinks I'm the world's best mother when it's the furthest thing from the truth. Thankfully we were saved by Rider and perhaps the worst live band I'd ever seen in my life.

I chuckle as I sit back on the couch, my morning coffee in my hands as I run last night through my mind. It was a pleasant night and I could almost feel the old pieces of mine and Judge's friendship slip into place. Not fully, never fully. Too much has gone on in the past to be able to go back to the way we were. All the hatred and anger I once held toward him is now only a glimmer of what it once was. Now I wait with bated breath for his. I'm sure he has questions, things he wants to know, anger at the situation or at me for not trying hard enough to tell him what we've been through. When his anger finally comes out it'll be in full force and rightly so. My stubbornness and inability to ask for help has hurt me once, and I know it'll hurt me again.

Sick of myself and going round in circles in my head, I haul ass from the couch, place my cup in the sink and leave, heading toward the farmhouse. It's so funny how small my world was three, no, four days ago. Just me and the twins. Six years ago it was just me, the twins and my dad. I shake off the sorrow and decide to get a little exercise, jogging up the stairs of the house, beelining for the nursery.

"There she is!" Remy smiles gently as I walk through the door.

"I got sick of being stuck in my head at home, decided this is better. There will be enough crazy conversation to keep me distracted."

"Worried about today?" Nat asks.

"Today, tomorrow, next week. It's my natural setting." I reply, snuggling down into a bean bag that is far too small for my ass.

"There really is no point worrying like that. You could die today. Or tomorrow."

"Thank you, Chewy." Ana rolls her eyes, her chubby son lying sideways on her lap poking Rosie, Nat's daughter.

"What? It's true. Do you ever see me worry about anything? Nope. Because I can only control what I can control," Chewy replies, petting her gator.

"Like Laney's brain development, and Rhodie's ass?" Blanche snorts.

67

"Exactly that. That's all I need to control to be happy."

She may have a point there. I have never once seen the woman flustered or upset. I, on the other hand, feel completely out of sorts. Everything still feels up in the air with the MC and Judge and everything they've got going on. Although we're all hoping today will put an end to it. As fun as it's been, I really want to get back to my own home, and the diner.

"Sounds like the men are getting ready to head out," Chewy says, head tilted, before she stands abruptly, scooping up Laney like a football, Chomper mirroring the position in her other arm.

"How does she know?" I whisper to Blanche as we follow her down the stairs.

"She has the hearing of a bat. And the nose of a bloodhound. I'm not sure if it's because she's neurodivergent or if it's a family thing." Blanche shrugs. "Pops is the same, but Tav can't hear a thing."

"Tav's hearing is as good as mine. If you think he can't hear you, he's lying." Chewy yells over her shoulder to us.

"That rat bastard," Blanche whispers. "Can't hear the baby my ass." She frowns, hoists her baby higher in her arms and speeds up. She's a woman on a mission as she storms toward her man, who is now looking pretty damn concerned.

I snort, then come to a stop on the deck. The whole of the DRMC are preparing to ride out. The Tombs' are loading up their SUVs and a big van named Truck Norris. The women with men are all hanging off them, hugging each other goodbye like Mira and Tank, or kissing passionately like Rhodie and Tuesday, their gator and daughter squished between them. Lovely is standing between Marx's outstretched legs as he leans on his bike and then I spot Judge. He's straddling his navy blue Harley, looking like damned sex on legs. He catches my gaze, giving me the crooked smile I've loved since I was five.

Weaving through the MC members who are milling around, I stop when the toes of my sneakers touch his big boot.

"Judge-"

"Leo."

"Huh?"

His eyes crinkle at my confusion. "It's Leo, Kai. I'm always Leo to you, OK?"

I huff, rolling my eyes. "Leo, be careful, yeah?"

He stares at me, his gaze boring into mine. "You talk like you'll miss me."

"It's not about me, Leo. There are two kids who have found their dad. They'll want him back in one piece."

"And you?"

I wrestle between what my mind says, and what my heart says. I mean, me and Leo, what we had is never going to happen again. But that doesn't mean we can't start to rebuild a friendship, one that revolves around happy memories and our children.

"You're gonna make me say it, ain't ya?" I huff out, hand on my hips.

His grin widens, and even though I can see the worry creasing his brow, at this moment he seems lighter than I've seen him since I arrived here.

"OK, fine!" I throw my hands up in the air, hamming it up, "Yes, I want you to come back too. In one piece. Unharmed. Got it?"

"Yes, Ma'am." He nods once as I step back.

Two bodies step in close on either side of me, and I know it's my heart, my kids.

69

Jax nods once at Leo, who does the same back, but Annie throws her arms around Leo's neck. Her light brown curls, identical to Leo's when he was younger, cover them both as they whisper to each other. He presses a kiss to the top of her head, and when he meets my gaze I watch as he blinks the tears from his eyes. The brothers all straddle their rides, the cacophony of sound builds as their engines start, the rumble moving through me, soothing my nerves. Marx circles his finger in the air, before slowing leading his men down the drive. Leo looks back, kisses his fingers and then holds them up in a wave. As if we're all connected, me and the kids do the same, not a word spoken. Annie-Bella sniffs, so I throw my arm over her shoulders, then do the same with Jax.

"He'll be fine, my love. He's a giant, tough man," I whisper in her ear, hoping to transfer some of my strength to my sweet girl, even though I can feel every fiber of my being screaming that it's too dangerous and that Leo should be here with us.

"But we only just found him," Annie whispers pitifully.

"We've survived this long without him, we'll be fine," Jax says flippantly, but his brow furrows in concern as well.

"Come on, there's nothing we can do hanging around out here," Nat says, snapping us out of our ever worsening mood.

Gravel crunching has me looking over my shoulder to find a fancy black town car coming our way.

"Oh goody! It's Dima!" Chewy exclaims. "This lockdown just got a helluva lot more fun."

"Mom?" Annie-Bella asks, big green eyes on mine.

"I'm sure whatever it is, it'll be fine."

Or at the very least, it'll be something that we can handle ourselves. Surely.

Pops

Shit. We've got Renae Sullivan on her way to us right now, the men are over three hours away dealing with cartel bullshit and it's the prospect, two young guys, two old guys and the women here.

I rub my hands together, readying my cache while the women fight about who is staying up here and who is going to hole up with the kids in the basement. I'm not sure how they'll sort that all out, and I don't much care.

"We're ready. Lovely will be up here with Mad Dog stationed in the kitchen, you're on the roof Pops, with TumTum on another. Got it?" Chewy barks at me. Me. The man who taught her all she knows.

"Yeah yeah, I got it. Just wait a moment, I have some goodies to set up around the house."

"Do it fast." She stalks off and I poke my tongue at her.

I jiggle the mount for my blow torch a little, making sure it's secure and stable. Don't want it falling to the ground or anything.

Kaia stomps past me, on her way to who knows where. "Hey, what's the problem, sweetheart?"

"Ugh," she grumbles, "I've been relegated to kid duty."

I try to hide my smirk, "And you want to be up here bringing the hurt?"

"Yes!" She jabs a finger in my direction. "They had *my* kids as targets. No way, nuh uh, am I putting up with that shit." She lets out a breath, her shoulders slumping.

"Well, it sucks you can't be up here, but you can help me if you want."

She narrows her eyes at me. I'm pretty sure I'm still on her shit list after the pepper incident. "How am I meant to help you?"

"You any good with booby traps?"

A grin slowly grows on her face and her eyes light up with a level of glee that I've only ever seen on Chewy when she's torturing.

"Got any small explosives and nails?"

Yes, I think she'll do nicely.

Chapter 7

Judge

"Something doesn't feel right," I mumble under my breath to no one in particular. All I know is that I feel itchy in my own skin.

"What? Could it be leaving your family behind while we camp out here ready to take out a whole damn gang house and cartel?" Rider asks, chewing gum loudly.

I glare at him. I knew it was coming, the teasing. I didn't mind when it was focussed on my other brothers who were falling for their ladies, but now I'm in the spotlight, I'll have to shut it down quick.

"I mean, I get it brother. That's the perfect little family unit. Not sure how you managed to pull that hottie though."

"She was my best friend," I growl. Ignoring my own advice to nip it in the bud.

"Ahh, playing the long game, heh?" He raises his brow at me. "So, how you gonna get back into her good books?"

"What makes you think I'm in the bad books?"

Tav snorts so damn hard that he starts coughing up a lung.

"What?" I swing on him, thumping his back with my hand, none too gently.

"Have you not seen the way that woman looks at you?" Tav asks with a strained voice.

I stare at him, because no, I haven't noticed. I've been avoiding all eye contact. It was bad enough when she was mad at me. Then disappointment crept in and now when I look at her all I see is shadows. I have no idea what the fuck she's been through, and I just don't know if we're at a point where I can even ask. I mean, it can't be that bad right? The kids seem pretty well adjusted, don't they?

"Dude, she looks at you like she wants to turn you to ash with her eyes," Vic Landry pipes up.

"Nah, she's stopped doing that now. I mean she still looks like she wants to punch something, just not him anymore." Rider grins.

"Can we fucking not talk about Kaia and the kids?" I growl, turning my back to watch the surveillance set up Tav's got going on.

"No, we have to talk about it. Because I can't stand to see my brother not get his woman," Rider pushes. Because he's a pushy fuck.

"What makes you think she's my woman?" I ask even though we all know what she is to me. I was hit with a bolt of lightning as soon as I saw her again. It was like my soul recognized hers. I keep that shit quiet because these rat bastards will be all over my ass if they knew my thoughts.

The room is silent for a beat as my brothers stare at me before they piss themselves laughing. Even the Landrys join in and they haven't been here long given they're prospecting along with Gus and Jules.

"Enough!" I roar, annoyed I let it go on this long. "Fuck's sake we're on a mission here. Let's get this shit done and then we can go home."

The dicks start making a high pitched "oooohhhh" noise and I'm about to tell them to all fuck off when Tav's phone starts vibrating all over the table.

"Pres?" Tav flicks it to speaker so we can all be briefed.

"Tell me what you see?" Marx barks down the line.

"Not a lot of anything. Cartel turned up, there's an almost silent party going on and pizza was delivered twenty minutes ago. Why?" Sniper asks.

There's curses down the line, "What are the odds that two cartels, in two different states, would be doing the same thing at the same time?"

Shit.

"Pack up and head home, something ain't fucking right." Marx barks and hangs up.

"Shit, Judge, you called it," Chris says, slapping a hand on my shoulder.

My gut kept my ass safe through all my deployments, it had me on edge at the diner when I knew something wasn't right. Shit, it's been calling the shots since the clubhouse was attacked. It's been one thing after another and now it's telling me that shit is going down at home and I need to be there.

We work as a well oiled machine, and I can't get over how the Landrys slip right in. They'll make good brothers and the thought of having another chapter to back us up can only be a good thing. Especially with all the shit the women we keep falling for bring our way.

"Fuck!" Tav says, not even packing his equipment away

nicely now. "Renae Sullivan and Serpiente are on their way to the farmhouse."

"What!?" What the fuck is going on? No, no, no, no, no.

"Dima called Marx, we need to fucking get there as soon as," Rider calmly states, moving with an efficiency I sometimes forget he has. He may come across as a goofy pain in the ass, but he's just as scary, if not scarier than most of us in the DRMC.

Straddling my bike I don't even wait for my brothers, there's fucking three hours between me and Kaia and the kids, and I've seen what these cartel fucks do to women. Jesus, Annie-Bella is only fourteen. Taking a deep breath I focus on getting myself to the farmhouse without getting killed or pulled over for speeding. I'm no help to them if I'm dead or in prison.

Glancing to the side I notice my brothers all have the same look of determination. They may not all have women and kids, but those women are their sisters, those kids their nieces and nephews. We're a family by choice and no fucker will bring them any harm. Leaning lower, I let the rumble of the engine soothe the beast for the meantime. The road melts away beneath my tires, my vision narrowing to only what's in front of me.

"How far away are you?" Remy's voice through our comms pulls me out of my thoughts, from where they had been rolling over in my brain for the past near two hours.

"We're another hour, at least," Rider replies, sharing a look with me. As road captain it's my job to get us to our destination safely.

"We need back up, Marx's team are twenty out, but we need more. We're surrounded and I don't know how long we'll be able to keep them back."

"Fuck!" Tav curses and rides up between me and Rider.

My gut screws up and I try to calculate the quickest, safest route.

"Judge?" Rider asks.

I hold up four fingers, then a fist. Rider nods once, getting the message. "Give us forty."

"Just get here!" Remy hangs up abruptly and I gun it.

I concentrate on my tires eating up the road, going as fast as we can safely go. Weaving in and out of traffic I raise my arm and indicate a turn off to a backroad that I saw on a map when I was plotting our ride here. It'd looked pretty quiet, off the main road but I'm hoping this way there will be less traffic meaning less danger. We want to get there fast, not dead. My brothers follow me, at my back as we roar through the backroads, cutting minutes off our journey.

Not paying attention to what my bluetooth is doing, I almost go to ground when Remy's voice patches in, "We're pinned down! Marx's team is stuck in the house, twelve blacked out vehicles are making their way through town. If you're on your way you better get here quick!"

My hands fist my handlebars as we hit the outskirts of Rose Grove. Knowing the town better than the cartel, we roar through the backstreets, headed straight for the farmhouse.

"They've just pulled in! Get. Here. Now!" Remy barks with more force than I could ever imagine her having. I guess working at the gym and running self defense classes with Dex has really paid off.

We're only moments behind the SUVs and as we pull into the long drive I spot them up ahead. The cocky fuckers are pouring out of their vehicles, cartel members and gang bangers working together to try and take us down. It'll be a fucking cold day in hell for that to happen. Excitement winds in my gut, clenching with anticipation. I may pussy out when it comes to dealing with Kaia and the kids, but I'll be fucked if I'll let anyone come in here and hurt my family.

I don't even wait for orders, pulling my gun and taking out anyone that doesn't look friendly. Some of my brothers head around the back, in case the house is surrounded, but I concentrate on the front and the front only. My gaze is fixed on the front door and I hope like hell that Kaia and the kids are in the bunker, safe and sound. The problem is, I know Kaia better than I know anyone, even with us being separated all these years. That woman is stubborn as all get out, and the fear I have coursing through my veins that she is actually not tucked away safe, is killing me.

I ride toward men, firing at will, watching with satisfaction as they drop, one by one. Some drop by my hand, others by the snipers sitting on the main roof and one of the cabins to my left. For some reason there are screaming men coming out the front door on fire, and I'm not sure how or why that's happening but I bet it has something to do with Pops. Or shit, even Elio. I don't know what they've done to the house, but there seems to be walking injured everywhere. The men who made it to the house seem to be running screaming from it in matters of moments.

Noticing a gangbanger scaling a side wall I head that way, gun raised to stop him from entering through the window to the dining room. My finger twitches on the trigger when he goes flying back into the bushes, screaming. Aiming my bike for him I notice blood the closer I get. I skid to an idle, staring down the barrel of my gun at a man who is full of nails and other shrapnel. His eyes are clenched shut, blood pouring from them, and it's a shame that he doesn't see my bullet coming. Revving my engine I blow dust over his body as I head around the side, eager to cut off any more brave fuckers who think to infiltrate the house my woman and kids are in. And that's what they are. *Mine.* I just have to convince them. Storming inside the house I move through the rooms as quickly as I can, clearing them as I come to them. Lovely and Blanche have Serpiente pinned to the dining room floor, and are in no need of my help so I move deeper into the house.

"Brother," Rhodie nods on his way past, a guy in a suit slung over his shoulder. "Your woman and the kids are in the bunker."

I slap his free shoulder appreciatively and make my way down to the basement as my brothers' voices ring out, stating the house is clear of any and all threats. It's been a fucking blood bath and I don't give a shit.

Entering the code that Marx briefed us on before we left, I wait for the door to swing open before stepping in.

"Hands up, motherfucker."

Kaia

"How much longer do you think we'll be here? Annie-Bella whispers.

"No need to whisper," Sage smiles at my daughter. "We're all in here together. But I'm hoping it's not for too long." Her eyes flick back to the screen that she's watching, where we can see everything that's happening.

Remy wired it up so we can be kept in the loop. We can see everything that is happening outside, but the house is a blind spot for us as Remy ran out of time to finish installing all the cameras. It's fine though, a little bit of information is better than none at all.

Looking around I take in how relaxed the kids all are. I'm not sure if they're used to this sort of thing, or if they just don't care. It's cozy down here, there are movies playing on the big screen, a playpen set up for the littler kids and the big little kids are busy working on what looks to be some type of wooden contraption. Mama Debs is busy baking with Mira and the rest of us are just trying to keep our nerve, I guess.

My eyes are glued to the screen as a crap load of SUVs pull into the drive. "Shit," I mutter under my breath. Men pour out of the cars, at least seven per vehicle, until it seems like a mob is on their way into the house. My thighs tense, and my gut drops knowing that Pops and TumTum can't put them all down before they get in. Then how much longer will it be until they find us? We've been assured that this place is bulletproof and next to impossible to infiltrate without knowing the code to get in, but what if they've got some fancy hacker like we do?

I extricate myself from Annie-Bella, who seems more relaxed now that Sage has drawn her into a conversation. It's good for her. With Chef upstairs helping keep the cartel at bay, Sage is doing pretty damn well holding it together for the rest of us.

Moving toward Mama Debs and where the other women have congregated, I sidle up to Nat, thinking if anyone was going to have a weapon, it'd be her.

"Hey, do you have a spare weapon" She stares at me with narrowed eyes, before a smile starts to form on her face.

"Ladies, Kaia is asking for a spare weapon," Nat calls over her shoulder, the women dropping what they were doing to gather around.

"Oh young one, follow me," Mama Debs says, wiping her hands on her apron.

I stare at Mira, Nat, Ana, Vi and Mama Debs, not sure why the hell they're all smiling goofily, but I'm sure I'll find out any moment now. They all file out of the kitchen, making their way down the long hall that separates the expansive living from the bedrooms. I take a quick peek back at my kids, Annie-Bella still on the couch with Sage, talking about who knows what, Jax standing sentinel in front of the large TV screen where he's been since we came down here. My chest clenches when I take in his large form. He walks around with the weight of the world on his shoulders, acting as the man of the house even when I've pushed him to be a teenager. Letting out a sigh I follow the excited whispers and chatter from the women ahead of me.

"You want weapons? We got weapons!" Vi explains, using Vanna White jazz hands as Mama Debs rolls open a pocket door that looks like a solid wall.

"Holy shitballs," I whisper, staring in awe at the weapons all filed neatly on the wall, kinda like I remember my dad's tools being kept in the garage.

"We got everything you could ever want!" Nat adds.

"Big guns, little guns, cross bows, ooohh look! A garotte!" Mira and her goldfish attention span starts petting all the weapons, muttering away to herself.

"So, what's your poison?" Mama Debs asks, brow raised.

A small smile tugs at my lips as my gaze locks back on to the cross bow. "Ahh, good choice *kotiro*," Mama Debs lifts it from the wall, handing it over with a handy quiver of bows. "Feel better now?"

"Much," I laugh as I strap the arrows to my back feeling like goddamn Katniss.

The other women take out a few items, all ranging from knuckle dusters to little single shot pistols. Feeling much more relaxed I head back to the living area, Jax still standing exactly where I left him. Shaking my head I move up to his side, wrapping my arm around his waist as it's been at least three years since I've been able to wrap my arm over his shoulders.

"How you getting on, buddy?"

He grunts, thinking over his words. It's moments like these where he reminds me so much of his father. "If they make it down here, we're fucked."

I hip check him. "Language!" I bark.

He rolls his eyes, then stares back at the screen. His eyes widen and I follow his gaze. There, larger than life is Leo, riding through the carnage, firing his gun at anyone that looks like a threat to the DRMC, to us.

"Holy shitballs," he whispers, clearly in awe of the man who fathered him.

Crap, so am I! He's fierce and strong and so damn sexy my thighs clench when he guns his Harley. He beelines to someone just off to the side of the screen, my eyes darting wildly to find him on one of the smaller feeds. There's some dickhead trying to scale the house, to make it through the window. The window Pops and I wired up. I lean forward, excitement fizzing in my veins. I jump when he gets blown off the side of the building with way more force than I was expecting, my gasp of surprise morphing into the giggles.

"Holy hell! Did you see that?" I shake Jax. "I need to get that on replay.

Jax stares at the screen as Leo pulls alongside the man, putting a bullet into him before riding away, blowing gravel and dust over the dead man. I stare, frozen in place. I knew that Leo wasn't a saint, but I never knew he would kill so easily. It just seems at odds with the man I remember, and the man I've met since I've been here at the farm. The Leo here seems almost hesitant, standoffish and unsure of himself. This Leo on the screen, this is more the man I remember. He makes his way to the front of the house and then he disappears. Just knowing that he's here, in one piece, has me feeling calmer than I expect.

I think that knowledge has the same effect on Jax too, as his shoulders slump a little. "Go grab a cookie, kiddo, while they're still hot."

He rolls his eyes. "I'm not a kiddo."

"You'll always be my baby boy," I tease, his eyes rolling so hard I'm afraid I may never see the bright green orbs ever again.

I stare at the TV screen, knowing full well that if Leo is in the house I won't get a glimpse of him. Flicking through the screens I can't help but feel a sense of pride at the sheer chaos that the DRMC has managed to rain down. I know that it's only been a few days, but regardless of what happens from here on out with Leo, I think these might be my people.

A metal on metal scraping sound has my back stiffening. Jax drops the cookie in his hand and flies across the room, standing with his back to the wall, next to the door, ready to pounce. Taking the cue from my son I move to stand directly in front of the door opening, feet planted, crossbow loaded and ready.

In my periphery the women, Sage and Annie-Bella gather up the babies from the play pen and move the Littles to the safe room deeper in the bunker. Flicking my eyes to Jax he gives me a tight nod. A gut dropping "click" rings out, the door disengaging. There is an agreed password that will be called out if it's one of the DRMC, and yet the silence is deafening.

Breathing out slowly, I try to calm my racing heart. I almost laugh when I notice Jax doing the same thing. It's funny how adrenaline screws with you like that. The door inches open slowly before big boots stomp in, coming to an abrupt stop.

"Hands up, motherfucker," Jax growls.

"It's me, Son," Leo's raspy voice fills the room and my crossbow drops, as if my arms couldn't hold the weight of it any longer.

My breath whooshes out of me before it rushes back in on a gasp, "Jax! Where the hell did you get that gun? Put it down, now!" I growl, burning a goddamn hole into my son's head.

Leo turns slowly, his large hand wrapping around the muzzle pointing directly at him. He holds it in his hand, not daring to move until Jax does first, dropping the gun quickly as if it's burnt him.

"Good man, you did good," Leo murmurs, resting this large hand on Jax's shoulder. My boy slumps into him and I can't help but rush him, hitting his stupid teenage boy shoulder before wrapping him in my arms.

"You are so fucking grounded for pulling a gun," I growl. He nods into my shoulder as I hold him tight.

"What did you think I was doing?" he mumbles.

"I thought you were going to hit him over the head with something! What the hell, where did you even get a gun?" I push him away from me, but not too far as my hands are fisting in his shirt so I can shake some damn sense into the boy.

Before I can get started on treating this kid like a rag doll, a heavy weight wraps around me, pulling me and my son into a warm solid wall, Leo's scent surrounding us. He stands there, holding us, until Jax and I feel as if we can stand on our own two feet.

"Where is Annie?" Leo asks gently.

"Shit!" I move as fast as I can to the safe room, hitting the intercom button, "It's safe! It's just Judge."

The door disengages and everyone comes flooding out, talking over each other for an update from Leo. Annie runs straight to him, wrapping her arms around his waist once she sees that he's fine. He looks momentarily shocked, before his posture softens and he wraps a large arm around her small body.

"What's the damage? Any casualties? Are our men OK?" Nat takes the lead, holding her daughter Rosie tighter, for comfort.

"The men are all fine, apart from Rider who got shot in the nipple."

As a collective we all stare at Leo. "He got shot in the chest? Is he OK?" Mama Debs asks, her normally tan face, pale.

"Not the chest. The nipple. It grazed past sideways or something. I actually have no idea."

I let out a breath, feeling better about that. Still puzzled, but at least no one got hurt.

"Roman's men and Moss Davies are doing clean up now. Someone will come get you when it's safe to let the kids up."

I nod, taking in the words. "Wait, Moss Davies, as in Sergeant Moss Davies?"

Leo gives me his crooked smile, but doesn't say a word. He gently removes Annie's arm from his waist, dropping a kiss to the top of her head, before handing her over to me. I wrap my arm around her and watch him walk out the door.

"Well, we better eat these cookies before Rider gets down here and acts all pitiful because his nipple got blown off," Mama Debs sighs.

A giggle bubbles up in my throat and bursts out before I can stop it. I snort and the giggling gets worse when my friends join in until we're all in a heap, leaning on each other, cackling.

"Ah shit, you heard the news already, didn't you?" Rider's voice booms over the sound of women losing their shit.

"Sorry 'bout your nips, Uncle Rider."

"Thanks, sweetheart. Can I have a cookie?"

Chapter 8

Judge

"The last of the kids Renae and the cartel had been keeping have been returned to their families," Marx announces, the table erupting with cheers, boots stomping, fists banging the worn wooden table.

It's been two weeks since we cleared out the scum. Cartel de Silencio and La Sombre Roja are now no more. Shit, even if they had some survivors across the border, their numbers have been decimated. Not to mention a little birdy named Roman may or may not have sent men down there in one last last sweep.

"In the last point of order," Marx looks toward Pops who gives a simple nod, "we need to make a decision. The compound is a total rebuild. It can be done, but at great expense and time. Pops has very generously offered to have the compound moved here."

Our shocked gazes all stare at Pops who starts to squirm in his seat. "Don't get all choked up about it. I have the space, and Dayz and I do our best work in my office here," he grumbles.

I try to hide my smile. He may act like a grumpy old shit,

but he has a heart of gold. His Love Pres lessons have been enlightening to say the least. I may not have won over the girl, just yet, but I at least feel like we're building something more akin to a friendship. Even if I have only seen her in passing this last week.

As soon as the cartel and Renae Sullivan were dealt with Kaia and the kids moved back home, not wanting the diner to be closed any longer than it had to be. Since reopening she's been working double time to get back to where she was and Tank and I have been busy as fuck catching up with Devil's Big Tow work. I've stopped by the diner for afternoon snacks and to see the kids, but I'm hoping to get into a better routine now that shit looks like it's calming down.

"Because the land is so expansive, and Pops says he doesn't need it all, it's been agreed to divvy up the area to build more housing, much like the Tombs cabins already here," Marx continues.

"Some of us will be adding on to the cabins," Tav adds.

Marx nods in his direction. "So, all those in favor of relocating the compound to the farm, say aye."

It's unanimous as everyone yells their agreement. The compound was home to the DRMC, but the farm is *home*. I have no other way to explain it.

"Good, we're all in agreement."

"What's the timeline?" Fox asks, healing well with rest and the love of a good man.

"The Landrys have friends, a crew that left the Keep not long after they did. Apparently they can get shit built or renovated fast, so we'll be bringing them in."

"Like those Amish barn builders," Rider pipes up. "I watch that shit all the time on TikTok, fucking impressive."

Pops stares at him for a beat. "You need to get laid, kid."

"I can't," Rider laments. "No woman is going to want a man with a dent in his ass and a missing nipple. I'm a nipless wonder." He throws his hands in the air before hitting us all with a glare. "I lost a nipple for you fuckers, the least you could do is give me the biggest room in the new clubhouse rebuild." His glare turns into a smirk until Marx throws his pen at him, bouncing it off his big head.

"We thank you for your service, brother. If there isn't anything else, Church closed. I got a woman to go see," he grins.

We jeer and give him shit, but it's nice to see Pres looking so fucking relaxed and happy. Lovely is good for him, and together they are a force to be reckoned with. I follow behind my brothers as we file out of the dining room, which is doubling up as Church for the meantime.

"Plans?" Tank asks, moving to follow me down the hall.

"Yeah, I gotta call by my parents."

He rolls his lips between his teeth, stopping on the veranda beside me. "Dude, I know you ain't dumb enough to not tell your Mom as soon as you found out you had a couple of kids out there."

He stares at me and I stare back, not breaking eye contact. "Holy shit, you haven't told them yet, have you?"

"I wanted to tell them in person, to their faces," even before my lame excuse has finished falling from my lips Tank is shaking his head wide-eyed.

"Your mom is gonna shit, dude. And your dad will just sit there, in his favourite chair, thinking. Not saying a word."

"You've been spending too much time with Rider. You've gone all dramatic," I grumble.

89

"Dude, have you forgotten who my ol lady is? I don't need Rider to influence me. I've got Mira." He grins wide, clearly thinking about his woman.

I ignore his gooey eyes and move to walk around him, stopping when he asks what time we're riding out. "We?" I raise a brow.

"You think I'm going to let *my* best friend ride all that way, breaking such life changing news to his parents, all alone?" he waves a hand at me with a shit-eating grin. "No way, I'm coming."

"Count me in too," Nitro's voice chimes in from behind me.

"Where are we going?" Rider grins, Tav, Sniper and Dex standing alongside him.

Rolling my eyes I stomp down the front steps. "Let me call Mom."

* * *

"Oh boys! It's so good to see you all!" I roll my eyes as Mom comes rushing out of the house, arms open wide, going from brother to brother giving them all mom-hugs, as if they don't get enough of them from Mama Debs.

"Don't judge her, you know she loves when you visit with the MC," Dad murmurs as he hugs me.

My whole life they have been the benchmark of a happy relationship for me. They met in high school, got married after college, then had me. They always wanted more kids but it wasn't in the cards for them, so I can see how mom would soak up all the attention my brothers give her. Even if it's because they're moochers and just want her cookies.

"Come on in! As soon as Leo called I got the oven on."

I swear Rider makes a whooping noise as he follows behind her like a dog. Dex, Sniper, Tav, Nitro and Tank following behind. They all crowd around the dining table, talking shit with Dad and pigging out on chocolate chip cookies. Jesus, Mom even has glasses filled with milk waiting on the table for them.

"So, what's going on?" Mom bumps her hip into mine before wrapping her arm around the base of my back as I stand back and watch the carnage.

"What makes you think something is going on?"

She raises a single brow and gives me a look. "You hardly ever visit, and now here you are, looking...happy."

"Huh?"

"You look happy. Which means I'm happy. So, do you have something to tell me?" She clasps her hands under her chin, looking just like Annie-Bella when she's trying to wrangle something out of her mother. Or me. I've learned that I have no discipline when it comes to the twins.

"Oh, he definitely has something to tell you," Rider says around a mouthful of cookie.

I give him the death glare and he grins back, chocolate chips all through his teeth. He isn't the only fucker staring either. Sniper is sitting in the corner quietly, a cookie in one hand, glass of milk in the other. Dex is ogling with the best of them, all while trying to block Tank from the snickerdoodles. The only brother minding his own goddamn business is Tav, who has become enamoured with Dad's train set collection.

Moving my gaze back to Mom's hopeful one, I let out a sigh, then move her closer to the dining table, gesturing her to take a seat.

"Chuck," mom hisses. "Leave the trains, *Judge-*" Mom winks at me, like she often does when she uses my road name, "has something to tell us," she wriggles in her seat, waving her hand at Dad to hurry up and sit his ass down.

Dad looks torn between Mom's eagerness to hear what I have to say, and talking to Tav about his collection. I decide to put him out of his misery and drop the bomb.

"Do you remember Kaia?"

"Oh I don't know." Mom gives Dad a look, "Do you mean Kaia Kennedy, your bestie from the ages of five through to eighteen? Lived right down the street? Had sleepovers in the fort, worked the summer job with you, was your date for prom? *That* Kaia?" Mom rolls her eyes.

I frown at her, a look that'll make most men shit their pants, and yet she sits there giving me sass. She reminds me so much of Annie-Bella. Small but mighty. Head full of light brown curls and body full of equal amounts sweetness and attitude.

"Yeah, OK, so you remember her."

"Oh, is she back in town?"

"You could say that," Tank mumbles, watching the show.

"Ah, yeah. She's in Rose Grove."

Mom claps, bouncing in her seat, "How wonderful! I always thought it was sad that you two lost touch," Dex snorts and then covers it with a cough. I'm going to kick his ass. Actually, I might kick all their asses.

I stare at Mom, ignoring the eyes on me. Just say it, Leo. Get it out. "Kaia has twins," I blurt, then stare wide-eyed at my parents.

"Oh that's so nice! What kind? Boy/boy? Girl/girl? Oh, a boy and a girl?"

"Yeah Leo, what kind are they?" Rider says, shoving a cookie in his big mouth.

"A boy and a girl. Jackson and Annie-Bella."

Mom and Dad freeze, confused looks on their faces. "That's an, ah, interesting choice of names," Mom says, suspiciously.

"Yeah, ain't they just?" Sniper mumbles and I can't believe that even my quiet brother wants to get a dig in.

"Um yeah, so the boy, Jax, Jackson, is named after me, and Annie-Bella is named after her grandmothers."

The silence is deafening until it's broken when the cookie Dad is dunking slips into his glass of milk with a plop.

"Her grandmothers?" Mom squeaks, looking equal parts hopeful and terrified.

"Come on man, put them out of their misery so Chuck can show me his stored collection of steam trains," Tav whines.

"I'm their father. Jackson and Annie-Bella are mine and Kaia's twins."

Mom blinks once, then twice before she launches out of her chair, aimed directly for my chest where she bounces off, slapping me and hopping from foot to foot, cackling.

"Oh my gosh! I'm a grandmother! Hear that, Chuck?" She spins to look at Dad, "We're grandparents! When do we get to meet them? Is Kaia feeling OK? Is she in the hospital here? I didn't even know you were back together!" She claps again, eyes shining bright, giddy with happiness.

My brothers are all sitting along the long side of the dining table, in a row, staring at us like we're specimens. I bet if the fuckers had popcorn they'd be in heaven.

"Ah, we're not back together, and Kaia isn't in hospital." I swallow thickly, knowing I have to rip the bandaid off. "The twins are fourteen."

93

Mom freezes, her eyes narrowing. Dad is still sitting frozen in his chair, staring into his milk, his cookie making air bubbles on the surface.

"You and Kaia. Together. Fourteen years ago? Wait, is that why she left town?" She frowns at me. "What did you do, Leo Charles Jackson?"

I cringe at the use of my full name and the words die on my tongue.

"Oh, oh! Pick me! I know!" Rider waves his hand in the air, the giant shit.

"Yes, please Rider, tell me why I'm only now just finding out that I have fourteen-year-old grandchildren?"

He sucks in a deep breath, palms flat on the table, "When Kaia went to tell him that she was knocked up she found him getting oral from one Chelsea Masters," he exhales.

"Don't forget the jocks," Tank unhelpfully adds.

"Oh yeah! One of the jocks called Kaia a name and instead of sticking up for her, Judge giggled. Giggled! Can you imagine?" Rider stares wide -eyed at Mom while my brothers heads ping pong between me and that fucking snitch Rider.

Mom turns very, very slowly back to me, almost bristling, and you know what? I deserve it. All her ire. "Chelsea Masters?" she says in a tone so low it makes my balls draw up. "That skank Chelsea Masters is the reason why I'm only now finding out that I'm a grandmother?"

"I think you'll find it was Chelsea Masters and Judge's hormones, ma'am," Tav adds unhelpfully.

Mom stares at me for so long I start to get scared. She's never quiet. Not like this.

"Show her the baby pictures man, that'll help," Sniper whispers.

94

I fumble with my phone, bringing up the picture of the twins in the hospital, little beanie hats on their heads. As soon as it comes up I shove it in Mom's face and take a big step back. Her face crumples as she takes in the sweet faces on the screen. Her finger traces their hats, before she looks at me with tears in her eyes.

"I don't care what you do, but you bring those babies and Kaia into this family, you hear me? If she has a husband, bring him too."

"She doesn't have a husband," I mumble back.

"Good. It'll make it easier for you to win her back. I never knew what happened all those years ago, but trust me Leo, you two were meant for each other."

My chest hurts and I know it's because Mom hit the nail on the head. I never knew I was missing anything in my life until Kaia walked back into it, full of piss and vinegar. Or what the brothers think is piss and vinegar. I know better. She isn't some ball buster, she's a little woman who does it to protect herself. Well, now she has me to do that for her, just like when we were kids.

I clear my throat, looking at Dad. He's a thinker like me, and he's been suspiciously quiet. "Dad, you got anything to add?"

He sits quietly, a calm port in the ocean. "What your mother said," he answers, picking up a cookie and shoving it into his mouth.

Mom hands back my phone, patting my chest. "You know what he's like. He's a deep thinker, that one. Give him two to five business days to process and he'll get back to you."

"Thanks, Mom," I whisper, bending to drop a kiss atop her curly head.

"You're welcome. Now get outta here, you have things to

do."

She's right. Next stop, Kaia's house.

Kaia

I flop back on the couch and stare at the ceiling fan. I should really clean that one day. Today, however, is definitely not the day. Who knew that spending six days at the DRMC farmhouse and closing the diner would mean that I'd have to work four times as hard to get stuff up and running again? Not me. I think if I were to do it all over again, I'd take my chances with the cartel. My feet are killing me, I'm sure my ankles have swollen to become cankles, and my ability to make small talk with people has flown out the window. Even the kids are exhausted and they're young, fresh youth. Imagine what it's like for my old ass.

I lean back into the couch pillows, wiggling a little to make a nice little groove for my body. It feels like a hug, and given that I haven't had a full body one of those for six years now, this is as good as it's going to get. I let my eyes droop, quietly listening to the still evening outside my open windows.

A rough bang at the door has me jolting upright, heart racing. My mind runs over plans and contingencies, a mental check box so I know I have everything where I need it to be.

"Kaia, it's me, Leo."

The adrenaline rushing through me stops as quickly as it started, and now annoyance takes a hold. Why the hell is he here this late? Crap, is he going to make me stand up and walk to open the door for him? I don't want to! I'm too tired.

"I know it's late, I just wanted to talk." He knocks gently again, "I could always throw pebbles at your window?"

I huff and force myself off the comfiest couch in the world, my bare feet slapping on the hardwood floors. I throw open the door to my big, annoying baby daddy.

"Do *not* throw anything at my windows Leo Jackson," I growl.

He grins that crooked smile I damn well like so much and the pain in my feet and legs almost goes away because the blood in them rushed to my lady parts. Traitors.

"Do you mind if I come in? I just wanted to see how the kids and your day went."

Ugh. He's so damn earnest and thoughtful and he is acting way less weird and skittish around me since the whole murdering people and the comforting us in the bunker thing, so I can't help but hold the door open wider, inviting him in.

I hobble my way back to the couch, and flop down in my usual spot, flicking a hand at the two spare armchairs in my lounge for him to sit. He rolls his eyes and stuffs himself into the chair Jax usually sits in. He stares down at it in disgust and I cover my snort with a cough.

"Is there a reason why you have such small furniture? Jax is only going to get bigger," he grumbles.

I shrug, "It is what it is, buddy. Maybe when the diner is doing a little better I'll go out and buy one of those huge leather man chairs guys like so much."

He stares at me intensely, "I'll have one delivered this week." I open my mouth to protest, "I'll also order a plush looking thing for Annie. I can't get her brother something and not get her something too."

I gape at Leo and the fact that he, on his own, realised that with twins you can't just get one of something. There has to be two, even at their age now.

"Thank you, they'll love that," I softly reply.

Leo nods once. "I visited my parents today."

I stiffen. I knew once Leo found out, that he'd tell his parents. I mean, they're great people and always wanted more children, but were only blessed the one time. The fact that they are now grandparents, well, they'll be over the moon. The only problem is that I kept the twins a secret from them, and now I feel like an extra shitty person. My kids could have had a family this whole time if I wasn't so goddamn angry and stubborn.

I'm jolted out of my thoughts by Leo's large, rough hand on my thigh. I really should have put proper pants on before I answered the door. Instead, I'm in a pair of boy short underpants and a DRMC tee that Pops gave me. I have no idea where he got all this DRMC merchandise from, but he basically kitted me and the kids out with full outfits - tees, hoodies, caps, keyrings, and who knows what else came in the DRMC tote bags. I didn't see any of the brothers wearing half this stuff, and Pops was a little shady on the details, so I can only imagine what he's been up to.

"Kaia, none of this was your fault, or my fault. It was just a shitty moment of miscommunication and our own stubborn ways."

"And your inability to check emails," I add on, with a smirk.

He rolls his eyes. "Yeah, that too. My parents understand, they just want to see you and meet the kids. Whenever you're ready of course," Leo leans back, holding his hands up in the air.

"Ugh it's just so embarrassing," I groan, covering my face with my hands. "They've known me since I was a child, then I go and get pregnant by you," I wave my hand at him and then slap it back on my face, "and then run away."

A rustling sound has me peeking through my fingers toward him, following his movements as he sits on the coffee table in front of me. He softly lifts my hands from my face.

"Why did you run away?" he asks quietly, his eyes flicking between mine.

I move to sit up, my feet on the floor between Leo's big boots. "When I came home from seeing you with-"

"Yup, no need to mention her name," Leo cringes.

"-them, anyway I was so upset I had to tell Dad what was going on. He gathered me up into his arms, and hugged me until I stopped crying. Then he broke it to me that Aunt Daisy - remember her? Well, she'd had a stroke and needed help. We packed up that night and drove the seven hours to her place. We nursed her until she passed away and by then the twins were so close to being due we just settled down there. Lived in Florida until we came to Rose Grove six months ago."

Leo runs a hand down his beard, nodding. He's quiet, which isn't anything unusual for him I guess. He's a lot like his dad, likes to process things in his mind before using his words. I could wait all night for him to speak, but there are things I want to know. Things I need to know.

"Why did you never return my messages? It wasn't just email, it was text too?" His green eyes meet mine, full of regret.

He sighs. "I lost my phone that day. It went into the river, along with all my contacts. I waited a couple of days for your temper to settle down, but when I went to find you to apologize, you'd already left."

"Why do we suck so much?"

He huffs out a laugh. "No idea, babe."

We sit in silence for a beat, before Leo's eyes find mine. "So is your dad still in Florida?"

"No, he ah, he passed away. Six years ago."

Chapter 9

Judge

Fuck. She's been doing this on her own for the past six years? I don't know what to say, so I just stare at her, hoping that she can read everything I want to say to her but just can't find the words. She has a dark look on her face, and it's not the first time I've noticed. I know I should ask, but it won't be just after I find out that her only parent passed away. She sniffs, pulling herself back together before giving me a tight smile. She's good at pretending, my woman, but not good enough. I want the whole story, but I can wait.

"Anyway, we decided it was time for a fresh start, so we came here. Close to where I grew up, but bigger, you know?" I nod. I do know. Rose Grove is larger and nicer than our little podunk town. "Um, while you're here, do you want to look at some pictures of the kids when they were little? I guess you have only seen the one I emailed you that time." She brushes everything off, and I'm thankful for it.

"Yeah, course," I say, trying to play it cool. Inside I crave seeing the twins, the life they've led, every little facet that I've imagined.

She grins at me and then bounces up off the couch, headed for the dining room. Her ass in those tiny shorts is visible under the hem of her oversized t-shirt and I try to not gape at her as it jiggles away from me. Clearly I don't try very hard, because my cock starts to thicken in my jeans. Kaia was always fucking hot, but now, with a little bit of softness and weight on her, she's stunning.

"Here it is!" She waves a laptop in the air.

All that does is cause her braless tits to jiggle under her shirt, pulling a groan out of me.

"Are you OK?"

"Yeah, just need to stretch, I, ah, spent a bit of time on the road today." Raising my arms above my head I swivel my hips so she can't see my wood. Fucking hell, it's like I'm a teenager again. Using my teenage tricks I hook my stiff cock into the waistband of my jeans, hoping that by angling it up it'll be less noticeable.

She plops herself down on the couch, patting the seat next to her awkwardly. "It'll be easier to see from here."

I nod, taking a seat next to her. She has one leg tucked up under her lush behind, her brown skin glistening in the warm lighting of her living room. I try not to sit too close, but she scoots closer, her knee touching mine, laptop placed between us.

"Um, I think this is the folder," she murmurs.

She clicks into it and immediately a picture of the kids smiling at the beach, arms around each other fills the screen. They look so happy and sunkissed, missing teeth and all. She flicks through to the next, then the next, pausing on each one, telling me what was happening that day or what she can remember. I laugh along with her, while all the time my stomach clenches knowing that I could have been there.

She comes to the last photo in the album, and it's a picture of her, lying on a hospital bed, IV drip in one arm, looking exhausted. There's a curtain cutting off the bottom part of her body, and a nurse stands on one side, holding one baby, her father on the other, holding the other twin. Frowning, I lean closer for a better look, realizing that she's in an operating theatre with the way everyone is dressed. Gloves, masks, those weird hats.

"What the fuck? Are you in *surgery* or something?" My eyes dart to hers in shock.

Her face screws up as she tries not to laugh in my face. And she better not, this shit isn't funny.

"Leo, I carried *twins*. Big ones because they took after their Daddy," my heart skips at her use of the word Daddy. "I had to wear slippers all day everyday because my feet were so swollen. Yes, I had a c-section to remove them. They knew fairly early on that I was too small to birth them naturally. They were born perfectly fine, and I was well and safe the whole time." She smiles at me gently, as if talking to one of the kids, but that still doesn't make me feel any better.

She was pregnant without me, her best friend and father of her children. She cried, she was afraid. She had fucking *surgery* to get my kids out. She raised them, first with her dad and then alone because I was too much of an idiot to check my emails. Fuck's sake.

A warm hand cups my cheek, turning my face toward hers. Shit, I wasn't even aware I was staring at my clenched fists.

"Leo, it's fine. They're OK. We're OK. Has it been easy? No. But I can tell you now, everything, every hardship, every challenge, it has all been worth it." Her eyes dart between mine, imploring me to understand, to listen. Not my strong point, but I'll try. "You'll find out that it's all worth it." Her thumb grazes my beard, tickling my cheek, before pulling away. I want to follow her hand, to have her touch me again but I hold back. I stare at her for what seems an age, so long that she looks a little uncomfortable. Thoughts bounce around my skull, none of them landing, so I blurt out the first thing that comes to mind.

"Can I see it?"

"Huh?" Her top lip lifts in the comical way it does when she's confused. I forgot it did that until now.

Clearing my throat, I ask again. "Can I see the scar? I just, I don't know, I just can't believe you went through that. That they got them out that way, I guess," I mumble, now knowing that it was an unhinged request.

"Out the sunroof," she snorts. Her eyes dart away before she blows out a breath. "OK, just, um, just know that I don't, um, I don't look like I did." She mumbles, holding her hands over her stomach.

I place my much larger hands over hers, almost covering her whole waist, "I think you look beautiful."

Pink stains her cheeks and she huffs, moving to stand in front of me. I gaze up at her and she narrows her eyes at me.

"Not a word about my belly, OK? I know I'm chonky and no one has seen it for -" she stops abruptly before looking away, "-ah, for a while. Besides, it's just a belly,"

"Breathe." She takes a deep breath at my command, then pulls her shirt up a little.

I stare at the fine, silvery lines that cover her lower abdomen, not expecting her to hook her thumb in her little shorts, and pull them down until I can see the top of the dark hair underneath her superhero panties. She reaches one hand down, pressing against her soft tummy and pulls upwards slightly, so I can see under the slight fold she has. There, hidden away, is a fine silvery line running from almost one hip, to the other.

Kaia

He doesn't breathe for the longest time and my cheeks begin to heat. I get that I'm not supermodel material or anything, but the least he could do is say something. I move to step back but Leo's large hands shoot up to grip my hips, stopping me. His eyes flick to mine before he slowly moves to his knees in front of me. One large, rough finger gently traces my c-section scar, before it's replaced by his soft, full lips.

He presses gentle kisses from one side to the other and if his hands weren't spanning my hips keeping me upright, I would have melted into a puddle at his feet.

"Leo, I-"

The words die on my lips as his bright green eyes stare up at me in awe, a tear trailing down his bearded cheek.

"Thank you, Kaia."

"What for?" I whisper, not trusting my voice.

"For giving me everything."

Reaching out a hand I lightly run it over his shaved head, the stubble prickling my hand as he leans in. I marvel at how we're so comfortable, as if we've remained best friends this whole time, and yet we're essentially strangers. I know he's been through some shit, and lord knows I have too. There's so much to say, so much to tell him, and yet it's all too heavy. It's not stuff you share with someone you've not seen in a decade and a half.

"Mom?" My head snaps to the stairwell at the sound of Annie-Bella's voice, "Who are you talking to?"

Leo moves to his feet gracefully, while I stumble back, landing on my ass on the couch. I'm a mess of emotions. Whatever just happened between Leo and I, it was like the world shifted just enough to knock me off my feet.

"Just me, sweetheart," Leo calls out, his eyes on me the whole time. He cups my face, skimming a thumb over my cheek before he takes a step back, craning his neck at the sound of the stampede coming down the stairs.

"Da-Leo!" Annie runs full force into him, almost knocking him off his feet as she throws her arms around his waist. "I *thought* I heard your voice," she beams up at him.

I marvel at how close they have gotten even with the two weeks we've been away from the farm. Ever since my ex, Annie has been hesitant around men. She's getting better, working at the diner. She's friendly and warm, but that's usually because her brother is always watching, two steps behind. I can still see the hesitation she has every now and then, I see how she'll quickly glance around to make sure Jax has her back. But with Leo? She's a total daddy's girl, like he's always been in her life. Same goes for the rest of the men from the DRMC. It's like she inherently knows she's safe. Hell, even Jax thrived under their attention, not looking at them with distrust like he usually does.

"I wanted to stop and check in." He smiles down at her.

She beams at him before shooing him to take a seat. He catches my eye and grins, doing exactly as she asks while she sits her little heinie next to me, curling up under my arm.

"Ugh, it's been a total ball ache." I shoot her a look and she grins unapologetically. I'll be having words with Rider, he's the only person I know who has been using that word every time he talks about his healing nipple and the dent in his ass. "But we have a soccer game on Saturday, so I'll take my aggression out on the field."

Leo barks out a laugh, and I roll my teeth between my lips, because clearly, he has no idea what Annie is like on the field.

"You are coming, right? It's mine and Jax's team." She grins at him as he raises his brow.

"You play with boys?" His voice lowers and his fist slowly balls up.

"Yeah. Rose Grove is too small to have a girls team, so Mom complained to whoever would listen and ripped the school a new one so I could play. They don't like it, but I don't care. And our coach is a woman so she's cool with it." Annie shrugs as if it's nothing.

Judging by the look on Leo's face, it is most definitely something. "And you play against other boys?"

"Yup. Wait, did you just growl?"

"Nope. But I'll be there." Leo manages to grit out, ignoring my shaking shoulders as I silently laugh.

"Oh oh! Why don't you come here first thing in the morning and we can all go together!" Annie pauses for a moment, "And maybe you could ask your parents to come too? I'd love to meet them. Oh this is such a good plan, I'm going to go through my baby albums and choose some photos for them to take home," Annie bounces up off the couch with way too much energy for someone who worked an eight hour shift alongside me.

Leo's eyes follow her up the stairs. He takes his phone out of his cut, thumbs flying over the screen before he shoves it away, a smirk playing on his lips.

My brows pull down, "What was that?"

"What was what?"

I wave my hand in a circle, in his direction, "That whole texting and then the evil smirk afterwards."

"Nothing," he shrugs one meaty shoulder, avoiding my eye contact. "I know that look, you've just done something."

His eyes flick to mine, a playful look crossing his face. "Maybe."

I inhale, about to unleash but then I think, "What the hell?" What's the worst that can happen? I've survived a Frozen Spiderman mashup five-year-old twin party with twenty-five guests. I can handle whatever he throws at me. But can he handle soccer day?

"Fine. Meet us here at 9am. We have to be there early to warm up."

"There's nowhere else I'd rather be." He grins, eyes flicking to the clock on the wall. "Time for bed, Kai," he moves to stand and my heart lurches a little hearing my old nickname fall from his lips like it never left them.

I follow behind his big frame on my tired feet, holding the door open as he moves to leave, spinning at the last moment. I stare up at his handsome face, the intensity something I remember from a fleeting moment in the past. Leaning forward he stops, just shy of pressing his lips to mine. His gaze flickers between mine, and I know he's giving me the power. The only problem is, once the anger and regret melted away, I was hit with the realization that I don't have any power when it comes to this man, especially not this version of him. Rolling onto my toes I close the distance between us, pressing my lips softly to his in barely a whisper of a kiss, but a heavy promise of something more. His lips curl beneath mine, and when I pull back he's beaming.

"Night, Kai." He presses his lips to my forehead, his large palm cradling the base of my neck, and then he's gone.

Chapter 10

Judge

P ulling up to the Kaia's in one of the DRMC SUV's, I picture myself walking through those front doors to my loving family waiting for me around the dining table, a meal laid out and whatever other shit happy families get up to. A smile stretches my face as my dream is about to become a reality. Slamming the car door behind me I follow the path to the front door, the picture in my mind of what's awaiting me clear as day.

"Door is unlocked, just come on in!" Kaia's voice yells from behind the bright yellow door.

Turning the handle I walk right in...to chaos. There are black and yellow sports uniform tops lying around, Kaia is using a blender in the kitchen while yelling at the kids, who are nowhere to be seen and her ass looks phenomenal in those tight black yoga pants women like to wear.

"Ah, are you OK?" I ask, shuffling into the kitchen.

I've seen women act like this before, so I know to hang back, out of the way of flying things.

She turns off the blender before spinning to face me, "Sorry about that, Saturday mornings are hectic as hell. I told you the plan, didn't I? The twins have a soccer game in about an hour –" she turns her head over her shoulder and continues, "AND THEY HAVEN'T GOTTEN THEIR SHIT TOGETHER YET!"

A rumble on the staircase foreshadows a goddamned stampede so I move my big ass to hug the wall, wanting to be out of the way.

"Hey Leo!" Annie bounces in, scooping up the smoothie cup Kaia has left for her in an obscenely large, pink thing with a metal straw sticking out of the top. "Thanks Mom! And Thanks Da-um Leo for my pink poofy chair, I love it!" She squeals at a pitch that I'm sure dogs from three blocks over can hear.

Jax follows close behind, tipping his chin, "Thanks for the chair, bruh," he gives me a crooked smirk before choosing to drink his smoothie straight from the blender jug.

I nod at the kids, chest a little tight that I've managed to provide something they needed. I wanted to show them I care about them and I know it's simple, but making them happy makes me feel about ten fucking feet tall.

"Get that in ya and then we need to get going. That smug bitch will never let me hear the end of it," Kaia mumbles the last part, my ears pricking up at that.

"Who's the smug bitch?" I ask, watching the kids drink their breakfasts, put on socks and generally rush from one side of the room to the other doing who knows what.

"Toby's mom and Mom's nemesis," Jax smirks.

"She's a total thundercunt. She's always trying to get the kids kicked offf the soccer team. Annie because she's a girl, and Jax because he's better than her crappy son," Kaia grumbles, moving around the kitchen with ease.

She has on one of those mom sports tops, it's in the team colors with "Kennedy" written across the top back. She then moves into the living room, scooping up bags, two fold out chairs, and a box of bottled water.

"Here, give me that," I roll my eyes, grabbing everything off her in one fell swoop. She stares at me for a long moment, before her lips tip up.

"I'm glad you could make it. Now, lets go watch the kids fuck up their opponent."

* * *

"Holy shit," Kaia whispers, taking in the DRMC setup.

When I told my brothers that I would be busy this morning watching the kids play soccer, I knew that they'd come out in full force. And full force they did. They've set up a pop up gazebo, there's a drinks stand, the women are all in black and yellow, the twins' team colors, and the men are sitting with beers in hand even though it's 9am. A stark contrast to the other soccer moms, who are all in athleisure (that's what Annie called it) with husbands who were probably good at sport once, but are now all fat, bald and dangerously red looking.

"Ah, if it's too much and you want to sit away from us, that's OK," I murmur, not wanting to embarrass her or the kids.

"What the hell are you talking about? This is awesome! Chelsea Wilson can bring it on!" Kaia makes her way over to the Ol Ladies, a huge grin on her face.

"Who the hell is Chelsea Wilson?" I ask the twins who, like their mom, are staring at the DRMC set up in awe.

"Mom's, nemesis, Toby Wilson's mom." Annie points to a chunky ginger with acne warming up on the field.

"Thinks he's hot shit because his dad played high school football and got a scholarship. Then blew his knee out and now he owns the carpet store in town," Jax adds, throwing his overly full backpack into the DRMC pop up gazebo.

"OK babies, I made you some energy bars, so get those into you quickly before you warm up. They'll keep you going," Mama Debs bustles over to the twins, tupperware container lid off, waving the bars in the kids' faces even though they both had smoothies about ten minutes ago.

Looking around, the DRMC bigger littles are over with some other kids their age. I'm not sure what they're doing, but I can see juice boxes changing hands as well as Elio writing something on a note pad. If they were any other kids, I'd think it was innocent. They aren't though, so I make a note to check in with them later. Moving my gaze around the field, the women are gathered together, babies on picnic blankets on the ground even though the morning is still a little cooler. My brows pinch when I realize Kaia isn't with the women anymore. Moving to walk around the gazebo, my eyes find her, gesticulating wildly at some tall, scarily thin blonde in one of those puffy vest things with spray on clothing underneath. A large, sweaty man steps up to join the conversation against my woman and my legs have me hurtling in their direction before I can even think about it.

"What's going on, Little Mama?" I murmur to Kaia, ignoring the disgusted look she gives me at the nickname.

"Oh, the usual. Chelsea and Roger here are bitching about the twins. Oh, and the MC." Kaia crosses her arms over her chest, her breasts instantly sitting higher, in the gaze of the big, red, sweaty guy.

Stepping in front of her to break his eye contact with her tits, I stare him down until he squirms. "What's your problem with the MC?"

He narrows his eyes at me, before they dart to the DRMC gazebo and back, "It's a kids' soccer game, no need for your type." He puffs himself up. All that does is turn him even redder in the face.

"My type has every right to be anywhere we like. We're going to stay and watch *my* kids," I glower.

"Wait, *your* kids?! I knew Annie-Bella and Jax were trash!" The blonde shrieks before her eyes grow wide. "Leo? Leo Jackson?"

"How the fuck do you know my name?" My eyes narrow and I don't recognise this awful bitch at all. No one calls my kids trash.

She throws her head back and cackles before staring me in the eyes, licking her pumped up lips obscenely. Kaia snorts loudly behind me and I take a step back as the scary blonde leans into me.

"Oh come on, Leo, you *know* who I am." Her gaze runs up and down my body as her husband starts making grumbling sounds behind her back.

"Yeah, Leo, don't you recognise your old flame?" Kaia teases, stepping up to my side, a smirk on her face.

Scary blonde runs a single red talon down the center of my chest, licking those goddamn shiny beach ball lips again. "Oh you know who I am. I sucked that soul of yours right out of your cock," she makes a slurping noise before cackling again.

"Jesus Christ, that's enough! Chelsea, we're leaving." Her husband grips her around her scrawny bicep, pulling her away. "Just keep your trash kids away from ours!"

114

Snapping my head to Kaia I wait for her to stop her hysterical laughter before I growl at her. "Who the fuck was that? And why the hell are you laughing so much?"

She calms slightly, wiping a tear from her eye. "That–" she jabs a finger in their direction, "–is your old girlfriend, Chelsea Masters."

I whirl back around in the direction they went trying to get another look before spinning and marching across the field, trying to catch up with Kaia and her short legs. "What the hell happened to her face? She blinked and her ears moved!" I hiss.

Kaia cackles as she stomps away from me, "Don't know, don't care. Obviously her carpet peddling husband makes too much money."

She comes to an abrupt stop, staring into the gazebo, directly at my parents who have come to support the twins. She jumps when I place my hands on her shoulders.

"Shit. Shit, shit, shit. What am I going to say to them Leo! I'm not prepared!" Her eyes are wide and the sassy woman from a moment ago is replaced by one on the verge of a meltdown.

"Look at me," I demand, turning her in my direction. "It's going to be fine. They understand. They just want to have a relationship with the twins, OK?" I choose not to tell her about the whole soulmates thing. She's only just started looking at me without trying to kill me with her eyes.

She squares her shoulders, head held high, taking a deep breath before letting it out.

"You got this, trust me."

Kaia

I definitely do not have this. At the time getting away from Leo seemed like the best thing to do. Having Aunt Daisy need help meant I could get out of town and get my head straight. Before I knew it I had been gone so long that coming back pregnant, with my tail between my legs was not an option. Stupid pride. Argh.

Leo leads me toward his parents, laughing with Pops and Mama Debs at the drinks stand. There are kids running around and I can see Leo's mom Annie's head swivelling this way and that, probably trying to find the twins in the mass of kids. Her gaze swings until it lands on me, her eyes growing wide as her hands raise, covering her mouth.

She stares a moment before rushing over to me, wrapping me in her arms, holding on tight like she used to when I was a kid after my mom died.

"I'm so sorry I never told you!" The words bubble up out of me as I cling to her, bursting into tears. She grips me tighter, rocking me from side to side.

"It's OK, Kaia. Leo explained everything. If he hadn't been a DUMBASS –" she says loudly over her shoulder, directed at her son, "you would have stayed and we would have helped you."

"I'm sorry," I whisper, pulling back to run my hands over my cheeks, sniffling pitifully.

"Sweetheart, you did what you had to, and what I've heard is that you did a fabulous job." Annie bends a little, her taller frame angling down so she can look me in the eye, a genuine smile stretching her face. "You did good, girl. Now, why don't you introduce me and Chuck to our grandbabies?"

I nod, wiping my face, once more, taking a deep breath and blowing out all the years of regret and fear over how Annie and Chuck would react. Instead of being pissed, Annie embraced me, and now I'm snuggled into the crook of Chuck's arm. Leo's soft gaze finds mine, his crooked smile playing on his lips. I exhale once more, looking around for the kids who are standing with Tank and Mira.

Catching their gazes I wave to them. Annie-Bella bounces over. I mean, why walk when you can bounce happily from one place to another? Jax lopes behind her, his long legs eating up the distance. They stop in front of me and before I can say a word Annie-Bella's eyes grow comically wide.

"You're my meemaw, aren't you?" she whispers. Annie nods at her, her lips quivering as she stares at Annie-Bella in wonder. "And you must be my gramps!" Annie-Bella says in a stronger voice.

"Yup, sweetheart, that's me." Chuck grins wide, chest puffed out with pride.

There's a pause, static in the air before Annie scoops my daughter up in her arms, Chuck doing the same with Jax who doesn't fight it. He leans into Chuck's large body, holding on tighter than I expected.

Jax and my father were close, closer than any two people I have ever met. When Dad passed away Jax struggled with his grief, his anger, his hurt. Watching him with Chuck heals something in me. We may have lost my dad, but Jax still has Leo's dad in his life. In actual fact, he has more than just Chuck. He has Pops and Mad Dog and I've seen how he behaves with them. It's like he's found a place, just like I felt at the farm.

There's some tears, and a lot of hugging. The DRMC all watch on with goofy smiles on their faces. It's clear that Leo and his

117

parents are well loved.

"See, wasn't as bad as you thought it would be, huh?" Lovely asks, nudging me with her shoulder as I watch the twins with Leo and his parents.

I roll my eyes, but then grin in her direction. As soon as I got here I was whisked away by the Girl Gang and I told them my fears. Obviously we did an intense advice circle. Some advice was great, some, like Chewy's, was a lot less helpful. I don't think moving away never to be seen again is a good option.

"So, ladies, I did a quick loop, and aside from that ginger kid's awful mom, there are three others who could be problematic." Blanche says, bouncing Tess in the front pack on her chest.

"What do you mean by 'problematic'?" I ask, brow raised.

"They're judgey assholes," Nat fills in for me.

Following where her finger is pointing, I let out a long groan. "Those are Chelsea's friends."

"Well, I have my eyes on them," Ana says, glaring in their direction. "They complained to that guy in the bright top."

"That's the ref. He can't really do anything about us spectators," I fill in. Clearly these women know nothing about soccer.

"Good. Because I helped put up this damned gazebo and I ain't packing it down." Vi says arms crossed over her chest, eyes narrowed at the bitches across the field.

"Does this kinda feel like high school all over again? And they're the popular girls?" Mira asks, coming to stand next to me, joining the stand off.

"Nope. I finished high school early." Chewy shrugs. "And I was younger than everyone by two years anyway. Unless they had the answer to the Bermuda Triangle, I wasn't interested."

Ana snorts, patting her friend on the shoulder, Chewy shrugging it off awkwardly.

"Ooh look! They're starting!"

Chapter 11

Judge

I'm going to be arrested. Kaia in her tight pants jiggling up and down in excitement, tits bouncing under her shirt, is pushing me to the edge. It seems I'm not the only one with eyes on Kaia, either, because half the soccer dads are drooling over her and if one more fucker looks her way I'm taking his eyes out.

"Yo, you look irritated to fuckery," Tank says, stepping up next to me.

"Do *not* look at Kaia. Keep your eyes on your own woman," I growl. I don't want to have to fight a brother.

"Why the hell would I be looking at your woman? Have you seen mine?" He gazes over at Mira, who instead of wearing a supporters shirt like the rest of the women, is wearing a dress with bumble bees all over it. I mean, the colors match the team I guess.

"Yeah, sorry brother, just too many fuckers with eyes on my woman."

"Does she *know* she's your woman yet?"

I glare at him, and then go back to staring daggers at yet another overweight fucker who dares to look at Kaia.

"You know, to make her yours you kinda have to use your words," Pops says, coming to stand next to me, eyes on the game. "Holy shit! Did you just see what your kid did?"

Of course I saw what Annie did. When my eyes aren't glued to Kaia, they're on the twins. They move as one. When one goes one way, the other moves opposite, always where they need to be. They've scored four goals together, and completely blocked the other team from gaining any ground. I can see now why Chelsea wants my kids off the team. They make everyone look like shit, especially their fat ginger kid who seems to throw his weight around a little too often.

"They're the best fucking players out there," I say to Pops, eyes on the play as Annie dribbles the ball toward the goal.

"Damn straight." He watches on a little more, but I know he's about to shit talk me, because he inches closer.

I really know shit's going to go down when Mad Dog moves in as well. "So, Son, you got a plan to win them over?" Mad Dog asks, not even wasting time on pleasantries.

I stare at them, hoping that if I don't respond, they'll fuck off. They don't. Instead they move right into my eye line, blocking my view of the twins.

"Do you mind?" I grumble.

"Not at all," Pops grins. "You know, if you want my help…"

"You just have to ask," Mad Dog says, slapping a hand on my shoulder. My eyes narrow to a squint, taking both of them in. "What? I'm helping him out."

"He's pretty much my VP," Pops answers.

"Your…VP?"

"Well, yeah, kid. I'm the Love Pres, he's the VP," Pops says

121

as if that makes sense.

"Say the word, and before you know it, that little lady is yours."

My eyes dart to Kaia where she's huddled between the women, laughing and clapping for the twins. I like seeing her relaxed like this. I like how she is when she has a group of people around her. She never had many friends growing up, but the DRMC can give her what she's always wanted. Friendship. A large family. I want her to have all that, and above all else, I want her to have me.

Turning to Pops and Mad Dog, I give them a nod. "OK. After the game, we'll talk."

They both give me nods, and move to the side to watch the game. Just in time for me to see that big ginger fucker run straight into Annie-Bella, knocking her completely off her feet, sending her smaller frame flying before she lands in a heap on the ground.

In the blink of an eye I'm moving like I'm back in some shitty sandbox, trying to get to one of my men. I drop down beside her, cradling her head. "Shit, sweetheart, let me look at you."

Kaia lands on her knees beside me moments later, brushing Annie's hair from her face.

"Step back! Let me see," Switch's loud as hell voice booms out, thank fuck my brother had a day off today. He's been pulling double shifts for the past two weeks, so it's good to see him.

"Gently roll her, brother," Switch gentles his voice as he leans in, brushing his hands over Annie-Bella's arms and legs. "OK, nothing seems to be broken."

At that, Kaia flies to her feet and starts yelling. Hers and Jax's voices break through my panic, but it's not enough for me to take my eyes off my little girl. I don't care that I haven't been in her life the past fourteen years. She's still my baby girl and some fucker hurt her. There'll be time for payback, I just need to know she's OK before I do anything. I run my hand over her hair, her steady breathing telling me she's going to be fine, but it's hard to focus on anything else. Behind me are voices I don't recognize, yelling, screaming, and snippets of voices I do recognize breaking through now and then.

"Whoa whoa, who do you think you're dealing with, young buck?" Pops voice drifts toward me, along with Mira's "Yeah!"

"What did you just call my gator?" Chewy's voice is dangerously low.

Shit. I turn in time to hear Ana yell, "Oh, it's on!"

The next thing I know the DRMC women are swarming. It's the only word to describe it. There's hair, bodies and fists flying everywhere.

"Um, Dad, can you please move out of the way so I can see?"

My eyes move down to stare into the big green eyes of my daughter, her words still working their way into my brain. Dad. She called me Dad. Swallowing thickly, I nod, moving my body and gently sitting her up, so she can see what belonging to the DRMC means.

My brothers are all standing in a line, arms crossed over their chests. Marx is in a yelling match with that ginger kid's father, Jules is staring daggers at another dad, and Pops is shoving someone's grandpa. The women are not holding back. Chewy shoves Chomper into Rhodie's arms, then hands Laney over to Sage who seems to be corralling the toddlers back to their play pen thing. Chewy then lets out a battle cry before punching one of the moms in her fake tit. Mira is pulling hair, Blanche is up in another's face and Vi has just slapped a mom, much to Jules

123

amusement. Judging by the look on his face, Mama Debs will be babysitting tonight.

"Holy shit," Jax whispers, under his breath. "This is insane." He turns his wide eyes to mine, then snorts. He snorts once more, before bursting into laughter. "And I thought Mom was the only crazy lady I knew."

"Son, never call them that. They'll have your balls," Tank says wisely, before moving to remove his woman's hands from the hair of some brunette she's fighting with.

A throat clears behind me, and the ref is there, Elio, Cove and Jovie standing in front of him. "Do any of these kids belong to you? They've been running a gambling ring and have won a large number of juice boxes that they're now selling from a stand."

I stare at the guy, then at the kids, then the chaos around me, before turning to stare at the twins. We burst into hysterical laughter and I just let the chaos wash over us. Someone else can deal with that shit.

Kaia

"I can't believe we had to forfeit the game all because of that fat bully kid," Ana grumbles.

Looking around, I want to burst into laughter at the absurdity of it all. The game may be over, but we're all still at the soccer field, chilling out under the DRMC branded pop up gazebo. These people are nuts, in the very best of ways.

"I'm just glad Sergeant Davies didn't have to arrest us all," I snort, then giggle.

"Nah," Vi waves a hand at me, "he would never. Mom would never allow it. Besides, we didn't throw the first punch. That scary blonde started it."

"To be fair, she didn't throw the first punch, it was more a slap," Nat says, holding a cold juice box to her cheek.

"Meh, tamayto, tomahto."

"I can't believe they called Chomper names. What monster calls an orphaned, disabled gator names?" Chewy glowers, and I can tell by the look on her face that she's planning something. Probably feeding them to her orphaned disabled gator.

It's weird, I should be creeped out that I'm building a friendship with a woman who has a pet gator that she treats like a baby, and yet somehow, that's one of the more normal facets of Chewy's character.

"I don't like unfinished business," Blanche murmurs.

"What do you mean? We totally finished that. I have the hair extensions to prove it," Lovely waves a handful of hair wefts in the air.

"What the hell are you going to do with those?" Nat asks, wide-eyed.

"Ohh, perhaps you could braid it? Or use it for crafting or something." Mira shrugs, eyes on the fake hair Lovely's waving around.

"What's your plan?" Pops narrows his eyes at Blanche, clearly calculating something.

"Well, it's not going to be the last game the twins play, so I say we tool up and come back next week."

We all stare at her for a beat before a smile breaks out over my face.

"Ah, why are you all smiling like that?" Leo frowns down at me in the fold out chair.

"Nothing," I smile sweetly back, then laugh out loud when his frown deepens. "Just planning something with the girls."

"And Pops," Pops adds.

"Yup, and Pops."

"Jesus Christ," Leo mutters under his breath the same time Marx does.

I suppress my giggle and gaze around at the scene around me. I mean, sure, some of us look slightly worse for wear, most of the girl gang's hair is a mess, because Chelsea and her posse are total hair pullers, but other than that, everyone looks happy and content. Jax and Annie-Bella are sitting with Leo's parents. Actually, sitting isn't really the word. Annie is almost on top of Leo's mom, that's how close she's sitting. Jax has his head bent next to Chuck's, busy showing him something on his phone.

"Thank you, baby," Leo murmurs, from above me before pressing a kiss to the top of my head.

Tipping my head back, I look at an upside down version of Leo, his green eyes sincere. "What's with the 'baby'?"

He raises a dark brow, that panty melting crooked smile tugging up. "Just felt right."

"OK. Baby." His eyes darken at my words and my thighs clench involuntarily. I didn't mean to cause that reaction, but now I have, I don't know what to do with it.

He doesn't move for the longest time, just stands there, staring down at me. Thoughtful. Or maybe calculating.

"Mom! Mom!" My head snaps towards Annie-Bella's voice, breaking the connection between Leo and me, but I'm thankful for it. There's so much he doesn't know, so much to learn, and I'm shitting myself thinking that once I tell him, he'll view me differently, he'll walk away and I'll lose everything I'm building. I'll lose the DRMC.

"Yes, baby?" I smirk at Leo when I use the term how I normally would, then switch my attention back to my twins, both of them bounding over.

"Gigi said that if it's OK with you, we can spend the night with her and Gramps!" Annie-Bella says, eyes shining bright. Ah, so it seems Annie Senior is a Gigi type of grandma. It brings a smile to my lips.

"But only if it's OK with you," Annie says gently, Chuck's hand on her shoulder. "Jax can sleep in Leo's old room, and Annie-Bella can have the guest room."

"Please, please," Annie-Bella whispers, her hands clasped under her chin.

I look at Jax, holding his gaze. Of the two of them he'll be the one I'll base my decision on. Annie-Bella is so desperate for family that she'd do anything to be able to stay with her grandparents. Jax though, he's spent so many years protecting us whether I wanted him to or not, that at any sign of his discomfort I'd put my foot down and take my daughter's moods and consequences. Jax's eyes dart between mine and his grandparents.

"Please Mom?" Jax asks. "Gramps has a collection of trains he wants to show me and I want to show him some videos of our old soccer games."

I look toward Leo, who's rolled his lips between his teeth, trying not to laugh. He'll soon figure out two against one is not as funny as he thinks it is.

"As long as it's OK?" I ask Leo's parents who look at me like I've lost my mind.

"Kaia, sweetheart, you know we love you, but you have to be missing your marbles if you think that we would say no to having our grandbabies stay the night," I try not to snort at

Leo's mom's very gentle way of telling me I'm an idiot.

"OK. Well, should we get going so you can pick up some spare cloth-"

"Already got bags packed, thanks Mom!" Annie-Bella says, grinning ear to ear.

My eyes narrow, "Did you plan this?"

"How would we have known that Gigi and Gramps would even be here today?" Jax answers, looking sweet as pie.

I move to swat his ass as he jumps away, laughing. "Too slow, Mom. Might wanna hone those skills before next week's smackdown."

"Do you want to keep them forever?" I ask Leo's parents, who nod eagerly, laughing along with everyone else."Fine, you can take them, and I'll pick them up tomorrow. Is that OK with you?"

"It's perfect, sweetheart. Thank you." I stand to give her a hug and she kisses my cheek. "Your mom would be proud of you," she whispers in my ear, before pushing me back and holding me at arm's length. "They both would."

I give her a smile, to hide my trembling bottom lip. Not well enough as Leo wraps his arm around me and kisses me on the temple.

"Judge, I do believe we need words." Pops gives him a serious look then tips his head sideways.

Leo lets out a deep breath, grumbles something about "Love Pres bullshit" and then wanders off, Mad Dog bringing up the rear.

"What is that about?" Lovely asks, looking around at us.

"Don't ask babe," Marx grumbles down at her, lips twitching.

"Anyhoo, now that two of the kids are sorted out, who wants to get sitters for the rest and have a girls night?" Nat asks.

"At the farm, of course," she adds quickly, glaring at Savage, daring him to say something.

I've had exactly one girls night in my life, and at that one I got to shoot a rocket launcher. Who knows what else we can get up to. "I'm in!" I yell, two hands up in the air.

"Dammit, woman!" Leo yells and I throw my head back and laugh.

Chapter 12

Judge

"**I**s it just me, or are things a little too quiet at the moment?" Rider asks, from his position on the recliner. Apparently shot asses and nipples deserve the best chair in the house.

"What the hell are you talking about?" Dex asks, from his position on the floor.

We're all hanging out in the living room of the farmhouse, which we're treating as a common room at this point. Since we made the decision to relocate the club here, we've been busy trying to reorganise the spaces. There are cabins being built on the property, close to the original Tombs ones, and there are also changes to the inside of the house. Church is in the dining room and chilling out is in here, with Pops' obscenely large TV. The wall between this room and the empty room next door will be pulled down to make a common room large enough to hold a growing club. Unfortunately, we still haven't gotten all the furniture delivered to make this room more comfortable, so the soft chairs and couches have already been taken. And if, like Dex, you don't want to stand, you have to sit on the floor.

"I'm just saying it's been weeks since we got rid of the last cartel member," Rider's eyes dart toward Sniper who stonewalls him completely, knowing full well that his brother is still alive in the new Rev Room, "and nothing. Not a whiff of trouble, which is weird because Judge has a kinda woman and they usually bring trouble."

We all stare at him. "What?"

"What?" he asks, confused that we're even questioning him.

"So, there were two big statements there, brother," Rhodie starts. "First off, you're whining because there *isn't* any trouble happening in our world, and second, you're accusing our women of bringing trouble with them."

"Yeah, that's exactly what I'm saying."

"Well, we're not one percenters, so it really doesn't make any sense that we should have trouble on our doorstep every damned week anyway," Wire points out.

"And yet, we do. Most of it is tied to the women," Rider replies."Well, except Kaia, but she hasn't been here long enough to bring drama,"

"I dunno brother, I would say turning up with two fully grown twins was pretty dramatic," Tank snorts.

"You leave my woman out of this!" I growl.

"You can't say that if you haven't claimed her yet." Pops says, rolling his eyes.

"I have a plan. I just have to take my time. She's skittish. Wary, like a rescue cat. If I come on too strong she'll run."

"After scratching your face up and shitting in your shoes," Savage snorts.

Rider looks thoughtful, tipping his beer bottle back, taking a large gulp. "Maybe she's skittish because she's going to drop a big ol' problem on our doorstep."

I scowl at him. Rider is a good brother, but he loves stirring shit. "She's not. She's just a normal woman. Nothing dangerous about her."

"Ah, I thought the same thing about Mira, dude. And that woman was being sent body parts," Tank shudders.

Tav snorts so hard he almost chokes. "Brother, there is nothing normal about Mira. You met her in a *jail* cell."

"That was a misunderstanding!" Tank jabs a finger in Tav's direction, "Besides, your woman ain't normal, either."

"Don't I know it," Tav grins. "She still has the highest kill rate of all the women." He looks all moony eyed and for not the first time I worry about his family's mental health.

"Yeah, I admit it, that was impressive as fuck watching her take out that cult." Dex lifts his chin at Tav.

"Look, I agree, the women we seem to attract do, more often than not, either bring trouble, or end up in trouble, but I can't be the only one who is enjoying the peace for a change," Gus says.

"We haven't had to shoot or maim anyone the past few weeks," Marx adds. "It's quite nice."

When I finished my time in the marines I figured I'd come home and lead a quiet life. I'd heard about the MC when I served a stint with Rhodie and it sounded just like what I needed to ease back into civilian life. We're not one percenters, so the lifestyle I was sold was we work together during the week and ride as brothers the rest of the time. It worked well until Chewy turned up. Since then it's been non-stop drama and assholes coming at us left, right and center. So I'm with Marx, it is nice to not be on guard. It's also nice that I've gotten to know Kaia and the kids. OK, it wasn't ideal at the start, locking them down, but we've been working on getting to know each other and it amazes me how only a few short weeks ago I never thought about my life outside of the MC, and now I have a woman and kids that I cannot picture my life without.

The thought that Kaia could be in trouble, or bring trouble, makes my chest tighten. I've seen the look on her face when she thinks I'm not watching her, the shadows in her eyes sometimes. I know it's a conversation we should have, but I'm just not sure now is the right time. I meant what I said, she's skittish as fuck. Comes across as badass, but it wouldn't take much to push her too hard, making her run again.

"Want me to do some digging, brother?" Wire dips his head toward mine, murmuring as the rest of my brothers argue over whose woman is the biggest pain in the ass.

I turn to stare at him, amazed that he never did in the first place. "Wait, didn't you check her before I brought her here?"

"Oh yeah, I did that. Not a deep dive though, just the stuff a quick search could throw up. She seemed mad enough as it was, I didn't want to make her even more stabby."

"Appreciate it, brother," I nod. "But I think if she's got anything going on in the background, I'd like to hear it from her lips."

He nods once, giving me a smile and then turning to rib Nitro about having the least problematic partner.

"Yeah, we all know I'm a total catch," Fox laughs. "But I'm with the Pres, I'm loving this quieter way of life. No trouble, no drama. Shit, the most drama we've had the past few weeks was that cat fight the women got into this morning," Fox snorts. "Did you see Chewy punch that woman in the tit?"

"Leave my woman out of this! She's a goddamned angel," Rhodie growls as the rest of us piss ourselves laughing.

"What the fuck is so funny?" Pops asks, equally as put out.

133

"Brothers, the fact that neither of you can see that Chewy is the queen of the crazies is beyond me," Rider shakes his head at his friend.

The girl gang's hooting and hollering drifts through the open window. There's popping noises and yahoos and I try not to laugh at the looks on my brothers' faces.

"Can anyone tell me, why the hell the women are out there with guns, living it up and we're all sitting around the living room like little old ladies?" Dom asks, looking from Vic and Chris to the rest of us.

We sit quietly for a beat. Then two. "Fuck it, you're right. I'm going out there," Marx growls, the rest of us following after.

We stomp along the porch in single file, looking like we're on a mission, but all we're going to do is gatecrash girls night. They're all crammed inside Chewy's house, and with the open door it doesn't take much for us to walk right in.

"What the fuck is going on here?"

Kaia

I jump at the sound of Leo's voice and crumple to the ground.

"Fuck, are you OK?" Leo's hands run over my body, and my alcohol fuelled brain wishes I was naked while he's doing it. Actually, no it doesn't, it wants to know why Leo ruined my trick shot.

I sit up, closing my eyes for a moment as I wait for things to focus. I have no idea what the hell Chewy put in the drinks, but those things are st-rong! Leo is still patting me down, feeling me up, whatever you want to call it and I slap his hands out of the way.

"Get off! I was working on my shot trick." I frown at my words. "I mean, tricksnot."

"Wow, she is *wasted*," someone chuckles. It's deep, so it could be any one of the hot giant men standing in front of me.

There's twelve of them. No, maybe fifteen. That sounds like a lot. I try to count them but the bastards keep dancing around. "Stop moving! I'm trying to cunt you. I mean count you," I giggle, tipping sideways dangerously.

"OK, well, let's get the gun out of her hands for starters," Switch yells way too loud, causing me to jump again.

"Why is it so loud? What did you put in the drinks, Chewy?" I loll my head to look at her. Or where I think she is, because she's dancing around a little as well. "Why is everyone dancing?"

"Chewy," a low growl sounds out, "what was in the drinks?"

Looking around I notice my friends are all in varying positions. Ana, somehow is upright, looking completely normal. So is Blanche who is playing darts, getting bullseyes over and over. Mira has a goofy smile on her face, Nat is passed out on the couch, and Vi is salsa dancing, trying to lure Jules into her hip swivelling web. It's working, because he's looking all frisky and smiley and I ain't never seen that man smile.

"What makes you think it was me that did anything to the drinks?" Chewy asks innocently.

"Pops was with us," Mad Dog points out.

"The whole time?" Chewy asks, brow raised.

The men all turn to glare at Pops who shrugs like his life isn't on the line. "It was a team effort."

Mira raises her hand, "He's right. We were all allowed to put one ingredient in the little drinky container."

"And what did you put in there, baby?" Tank asks gently.

135

"I put in the secret ingredient," she says in a loud voice and not the whisper she was going for.

"And what was that?" Marx asks, holding a goofy smiling Lovely upright.

"The stuff in the vial," Mira giggles, then her head rolls back and a loud snore comes out of her.

"Wait, what stuff in the vial?" Pops and Chewy ask in unison. It's so creepy funny that a giggle bursts out of me.

"Huh?" Mira asks, lids half closed.

"Baby," Tank says gently, "what vial?"

"Oohh that pretty green one, so vibrant," she whispers, patting her boobs, most likely looking for her pad and pen.

Chewy and Pops share a look and the room is silent save for Blanche's darts hitting the dart board.

"Chewy, what was in the pretty green stuff?" Marx growls so low I edge closer to Leo, so I'm not collateral damage when he blows.

"Oh, it was just absinthe," she says at the same time Pops says, "Just a bit of herbal ecstasy".

Blanche's rhythmic darts throwing stops and everyone stares at each other before Chewy yells "Run!" and for some reason, the whole girl gang follow her lead and we bolt.

Well, some of us do. Chewy clambers over the couch only to be caught midair by Rhodie. Lovely looked like she was going to run, but given that Marx is holding her up I don't think it's going to happen. Nat is still asleep on the couch, Vi has shimmied her way straight to Jules and Ana ran right out the back door with Gus hot on her heels.

"I do not run." Mira slurs, as she power walks out the door with Tank shaking his head, following her at his normal pace.

"What you gonna do, Little Mama?" Leo growls down at me,

136

a glint in his eye.

I purse my lips and think about it. Can I outrun him? No. Do I have a primal kink? I'm not sure, but I guess I could find out.

"What the hell is a primal kink?" Sniper mutters and my eyes grow wide.

"Yes, Kai, you said that all out loud," Leo says, arms folded across his big, poofy chest, lips twitching.

"Shit," I whisper, then I take off as fast as my legs can go. Which isn't that fast given that I'm short and stubby and haven't run since high school.

I dodge the brothers that don't have women to chase, and I take their laughter and cheering to mean that I am totally winning. Totally. Until I'm horizontal, my legs still running but I'm in the air.

"Come on, let's get you sobered up and into bed. You're gonna feel it tomorrow, baby," Leo's voice is light and apparently so am I as he carries me like a misbehaving toddler into the trailer me and kids called home not long ago.

"Oh, I miss you trailer. I miss you ugly greige couch. I miss you - oomph," I glare at Leo as I hit the bed.

He stomps out of the room, returning quickly with a huge glass of water and some Tylenol. "Swallow. Drink. Then sleep, in that order."

"Huh, funny, Usually it's drink, swallow-" I give him my most seductive look and a bleary wink, "then sleep."

Leo snorts, grips my hand, and wraps it around the water glass, tipping it to my lips slightly. I exhale loudly, then guzzle it down in one go, just to be sassy.

"Good girl," Leo murmurs, pressing a kiss to my forehead and essentially making me melt into a puddle on the bed. "Come on, let's get you into bed so you can get some sleep."

He pulls back the covers, then kneels at my feet, gently removing my shoes one by one, then my socks. He grins at my pink toenails, then moves to stand, gently maneuvering me into bed, my head hitting the soft pillow as he tucks me in. Tears prick my eyes at the care he is giving me. It's been a long time since anyone treated me this gently. He presses a kiss to my temple, running a hand over my hair.

He straightens and moves to turn, but I stop him by grabbing his hand. "Stay with me. Please?" My voice comes out smaller than I want it to, but it doesn't matter. Leo would still know how I was feeling just from one look.

"If I get in that bed, you're mine. I mean it, Kai, you're mine. All of you." His green eyes bore into mine in the low light, and I can't think of anything I want more, than to be his.

My voice doesn't work, probably because I'm busy gaping at him, so instead, I nod. The tension he was holding leaves his body, his shoulders dropping, a smile playing on his lips. He doesn't say another word, just moves to the other side of the bed, and undresses until he's in his boxer briefs. I stare in awe that this man, this fine specimen, wants me. His skin is decorated in black tattoos, his chest, ribs, arms and stomach all inked artfully. He has muscles on muscles, and just the right amount of chest hair.

"Holy shit, I've died and gone to heaven," I whisper.

The bed dips where he joins me, rolling me to face away from him as he curls his larger body around mine. "No baby, it's me that is in heaven."

Chapter 13

Judge

F uck. If she doesn't stop whining in her sleep and grinding that soft, sweet ass against me, I'm going to either blow in my boxers like a teenager, or wake her up and fuck her into the mattress. It's been a long while since the last time I picked up a piece, growing tired of nameless faceless women at parties. Not to mention we've been a little busy with all the shit that's been coming our way. It didn't really seem like a good time to go out picking up women. On one hand, I'm glad. With Kaia back in my life the last thing I need is some hangaround causing trouble. On the other hand, it's been such a long time for me that I don't think I'd last long even if I wanted to do anything with Kaia. Looks like blowing my load in my shorts is inevitable.

"Mmmm, Leo. Do. Not. Move. Don't even think about it," Kaia says, angling her ass just enough for me to feel the sweet heat between her legs.

My hand wraps around her hip, holding her still, "Baby, if you keep doing that I'm going to tear those little panties off and fuck you senseless."

She freezes for a minute, the only sound in the room is Kaia's heavy breathing. She rolls slowly toward me, a smirk on her face and pure fucking mischief in her eyes.

"Oh really? What would you do if I did this?" she sits up on her knees and before I can even open my mouth to say something she peels her top off, leaving her sitting in a bright purple bra. One of those see through ones. That's important to know because I'm eye to eye with her dark berry-colored nipples, that are just begging to be in my mouth.

I swallow thickly. It wasn't that many hours ago this woman was off her tits on absinthe and herbal ecstacy. She's bound to not be in her right mind, but Jesus watching her stand on the bed and slowly peeling her panties down is pushing me to my limit.

"Babe, how about you pop those back on and let's get you another glass of water, hmm? Just to sober you up a little." As much as I want her, I can't in all good conscience, take her when she's not sound of mind or whatever the words are.

"Huh?" Her lip curls up as she looks down at me. She looks fucking adorable. And mad. "What the hell Leo? You can't threaten to fuck me senseless and then take it back! Is it my body?" she looks down at her soft belly, sucking it in, then looking behind her at that fantastic ass.

I sit up, reaching for her hands. "Babe, it's not about the belly or the ass, I'm fucking hard as steel looking at you. It's about how you're still drunk and I'm not fucking you when you're not with me, on the level, with everything we do."

"What the hell are you talking about? I'm perfectly fine. I get that I was pretty tipsy last night, but I'm completely sober. Whatever the hell Pops and Chewy put in those drinks is magic because I feel pretty good." She shrugs, then frowns at me. "You're an ass."

She walks that sweet ass to the end of the bed, before stepping off the end, moving to pick up her clothes, looking through her pockets.

"What are you doing?"

"Looking for my phone." She finds it, and presses the button to wake it up, checking the time. She throws it on the bedside then waltzes right out of the room.

I lie there, staring out the door, cock still at full mast. What the hell just happened? One minute she was hot for me, the next, in the kitchen. OK, I get that it was my fault for ruining the mood, but still, I definitely thought she was coming back to bed. What the hell do I do?

I peek out the door, trying to get a glimpse of what she's doing out there. It's loud, and there seems to be some banging, but I can't make out what that could mean. Shit. I've messed this up and I have no idea how to get us back on track. Not just because my dick wants to get wet, but because it feels like I ruined a moment and I have no idea how to get it back. I could go out there and be all manly alpha, or I could just continue to sit here and wait for her to come back. If she comes back. A door slams and the shower starts up, the running water loud in the silent trailer. I sit for another beat and then realize I'm going to have to ask for advice. Dammit.

Leaning over I stretch to pick my jeans up from the floor, pulling my phone from my pocket and speed dialling the one person who can help me.

"Kid?"

"Pops, I need your help."

"Why are you whispering?" he yells back.

"I did something and Kaia stomped out of the room and now she's in the shower."

There's silence on the other end of the phone. "Did you do something to hurt her?" Pops' tone is menacing, slow and low.

"No! I tried *not* to hurt her!"

"Explain!"

I run my hand down my face. I can't believe I'm going to have to say this shit out loud. "We woke up feeling...amorous. I told her if she didn't stop teasing me I'd hmmm her."

"You'd what?"

"Hmm her. You know, make love to her." I shake my head, "Anyway, she called my bluff and started getting, ah, *comfortable*,"

"Comfortable?"

"You know, when women in those old movies say 'let me change into something a little more *comfortable*'?"

"Kid, I have no idea what the fuck you're saying other than you're sounding like a fucking prude."

"Ugh, look, she got more *comfortable* and then I realized that maybe she was still drunk from last night and I didn't want to, ah, make love to her until she was in her right mind and in control of her actions."

It's silent on the line again, then a long, drawn out sigh. "You're an idiot. The drinks are specially formulated to burn off fast. No hangovers. It's been at least nine hours since she had the last one. That woman was in her right mind and wanted your dumb ass. She's probably in the shower embarrassed as fuck."

I flop back onto the bed, groaning. Why am I always fucking this up?

"Judge?"

"Yeah?"

"Go fix it! Jesus Christ," he keeps mumbling right up until the point he hangs up on me.

And then I hear something. A whimper. Then another, coming from the bathroom and my gut clenches, chest tightening. I did that. I doubted Kaia's word, then I made her feel bad about herself. She's probably in there right now, looking at her beautiful body with nothing but contempt because she has scars and stretch marks. Things that make her infinitely more beautiful in my eyes and I've made her feel less than.

Another whimper sounds out and I can't take it anymore. My feet eat up the distance between us. I don't knock, I just walk straight in, coming to a complete stop when another whimper leaves her lips, then a long shuddering moan as she pants through her orgasm, showerhead pointed directly at the promised land.

"Out. Now."

Kaia

A growl echoes through the bathroom and I freeze in my post orgasmic haze.

"Out. Now."

I freeze, water still hitting my clit at full force, my core clenching as my legs begin to shake with another impending orgasm. I hold Leo's eye contact as my peak builds. He takes one step toward me, his body heaving as if he's run a marathon while I was in here ridding myself of the pent up sexual tension. His breathing is labored, as if watching me bring myself to

143

completion is painful for him. Running my gaze down his body and seeing the purple head of his cock peeking out from the top of his boxer shorts, maybe it is.

The light in the bathroom glistens off a small wet patch on his lower belly, the dark hair matted from where his cock is leaking precum. Just the thought of running my mouth over that patch, tasting his essence on my tongue has my peak hitting me at full force, stealing the breath from my lungs.

"Dammit, Kaia!"

He rips the shower head from my hand, shuts off the water and throws me dripping wet over his shoulder.

"Stubborn fucking woman, I thought I'd fucking hurt you with my words, refusing to fuck you, whimpering in here like I broke your damn heart and instead you're playing with that pretty pussy," he mutters under his breath, spanking my wet ass in punishment.

My ass burns for a moment before Leo's rough palm soothes the sting, his long fingers dipping between my legs, sliding easily into my wet hole, my muscles clenching around his fingers.

"Fuuuuck baby, your greedy little pussy is aching to be filled."

I whimper at his words and wonder why the hell it's taking us so long to get to the bedroom until I recognize the carpet under foot. I brace myself to be tossed onto the bed, however typical Leo doesn't do that. Instead he gently maneuvers me off his shoulder, somehow flipping me around until I'm in his arms, bridal style. He places one knee on the bed, then the other, shuffling us until he's able to gently lay me down, my head on the pillow.

He gazes down at me with heat in his eyes, goosebumps

breaking out over my skin. I'm unsure if it's from the look he's giving me or the cool air drying my skin. He runs a hand from my throat, down between my breasts and over my stomach before moving to my thigh, slowly, reverently.

"I never in a million years thought I'd ever get the chance to see you like this ever again," he whispers, voice raw.

I roll my eyes, trying to lighten the heaviness of his words. "Like you thought about me while you were out sowing your wild oats."

His large palm rests on my thigh, his rough thumb rubbing just inside my thigh. Not sexual, and yet, it seems to be ramping up my desire nonetheless.

"I thought about you more than was good for me," he murmurs.

My hand moves of its own accord, cupping his cheek, his beard rough on my skin. "I thought about you too," I whisper, not wanting to speak too loudly and ruin whatever this is bubbling between us.

Yes, Leo is handsome and sexy as fuck. But our past is so messy, so beautiful and I'm realizing now, unfinished. I may have shouted from the rooftops that I didn't want anything to do with Leo Jackson, but I'm starting to realize that he's a part of me, just like our twins.

He snorts. "Your thoughts would have been cursing my name." He leans forward and nips at the underside of my breast.

I suck in a breath, "Not always. Sometimes I thought about our sleepovers in the treehouse. How excited we were when our parents let us go to the diner unsupervised. The time we practiced kissing."

He snorts again, his shoulders shaking with his laughter.

"That was pretty memorable."

I grin up at him. "Yeah, I think I'm a little better now."

His lids lower as his eyes dart between my eyes and my lips. He leans from the waist, looming over me and I can't wait to feel the weight of him as he presses me into the mattress. His lips meet mine, soft, gentle. One swipe of his tongue and I allow him entrance. As soon as my tongue slides against his he pins me to the bed with his weight and I welcome it, welcome him as he settles between my spread thighs.

Moaning into the kiss I run my hands over his body, surprised by the firmness of his bulk.

He pulls away, sucking in a breath before peppering my face, throat, collarbone with kisses. "I've thought about pinning you down and kissing you senseless ever since you came at me and kicked me out of your diner."

I chuckle, covering my face with my hands, "Did I ever apologize for that?"

"No need, sweetheart, you were protecting yourself." He kisses the top of my breast, cupping it in his large hand.

"Damn straight, I've been protecting myself and those kids for a while now," I say lightly, covering up the depth of what's happened to me, to the kids.

"You don't have to anymore, I've got you. I've always got you." He stares deep into my eyes and I try to convey how much I want that to be true.

He gives me that crooked grin I love so much before leaning down and kissing me again in earnest. My body zings like a live wire, having not long ago orgasmed I can feel myself working up again, my pussy clenching with the need to be filled by the man on top of me. Leo takes one look at me and as always, he knows what I need. With a smirk he moves down my body, cupping beneath my breast and raising it to his mouth, a gentle lick on my nipple has my body bowing. That one movement is like a red flag to a bull as Leo *feasts* on me, alternating between nibbling, licking and sucking my sensitive buds.

I gaze down my body, his hooded eyes holding mine as he pulls back and bats my tight nipple with this tongue. My hips grind upwards, riding his rock hard abs, trying to get some type of purchase, some type of pressure where I need it.

"I've got you, Kai, always," he whispers, moving his body lower, kissing my belly, my stretchmarks, my scar.

He settles between my legs, his thick fingers spreading my sex wide before he dives in and eats me like a starving man. It's all too much and not enough as he laps at me before sucking my clit into his mouth, his rhythmic suction has me falling over the edge. My body bows off the bed, stars bursting behind my eyes as an orgasm shocks me, barreling into me like a freight train, so sudden, so powerful.

"Fucking delicious," Leo growls, rising to his knees, his rough hands gripping the inside of my thighs, spreading me further open for his bulk until it's almost painful.

He rubs the head of his cock against my folds, pressing into me slightly before pulling me away, then doing it again, pressing his mushroom head into my still clenching sex.

"Leo," I pant, unable to articulate any other words.

"I've got no condom, baby, but I'm clean, I've not been with anyone in a long time, and my physical came back clear."

I really want that dick, but this is important. "I'm clean too, and I have an IUD," something passes over Leo's face. Was that disappointment?

Before I can decipher what it was, he presses into me, my walls screaming as they try hard to accommodate his girth.

147

"I know, baby. Just breathe." He holds himself still, waiting for me to adjust to his size. I definitely do not remember Leo being this big. Or maybe he was and I just hadn't seen enough dicks to be able to judge. Ha. Judge. Dammit, his dick is making me drunk. "You OK for me to move, Kai?" His voice is tight and a laugh bubbles up, causing me to clench around him, making both of us groan.

"Please," I gasp, not knowing whether I want him to move or stay still.

He takes it to mean move and my god, every nerve ending comes alive as his thick cock hits all the pleasure points inside me. His groan is low and gravelly as he pumps long and slow into me. The steady thrusts driving me to madness.

"Leo, more, harder," I manage to grit out.

He grunts once, moving his hands under my ass, angling my hips up just a little before powering into me.

"Holy fuck!"

Chapter 14

Judge

Kaia screams as I bottom out deep inside her, her perfect pussy gripping me like she never wants to let me go. The memories of the times we made love all come rushing back in a flood of emotion. Never has it felt this good with anyone but Kaia. The connection between us is unreal as I power in and out of her. Her pleas and cries for more and harder bounce around the walls along with the sound of our skin slapping, coming together as one. I want this to last forever, for as long as I live, and yet I know from the telltale tingle in my spine that it'll be over soon. I can only hope that once the post orgasmic glow has worn off that she doesn't run. But I have a plan for that. I will chase her and fuck her into submission.

Pulling out of her and pinching the base of my dick, I roll to my back and lift her limp body over mine, her back to my chest, her short legs flopping on either side of mine. Reaching down I grip my hard cock, nestle it into her dripping hole, and power up into her from below. Her head lolls on my shoulder as

I nibble her ear lobe, her moans turning into cries as I hold her to me, one arm banded around her waist, the other wrapped across her chest, hand resting gently at her throat.

"Give me one more baby, just one more and I'll fill you with my cum." She gasps, her feet finding purchase on the bed so she can bear that hot little pussy down on me.

I power into her over and over again until her thighs lock tight and her body trembles in ecstasy. Only then do I release with a long, low groan, my body joining hers in rhythmic shudders.

"I've never," she swallows. "It's never been like that with anyone but you," she whispers, and then whimpers, a sob ripping from deep inside her, her tears tracking down the side of her face, pooling on my chest.

"I know, Kai. It's the same for me." I press kisses to the side of her head, her tears salty on my lips.

We lie like this for long moments, my softening cock still warm and wet inside her, as she lays in my arms, back to my chest. I breathe her in, all her scents. The green apple of her shampoo, the drying sweat on her skin, the sweet tang of her pussy still lingering in my beard.

She rolls off me, and I instantly feel the loss of our connection. I reach for her, but she sniffles and shimmies off the bed, thighs clenched as she runs to the next room to clean up. My lips twitch as I'm hurtled back to the past, the very first time I made fumbling love to her so we could lose our virginities to someone we trusted. I ran a bath and prepared a washcloth to clean her up, after reading about it in one of my mom's romance novels I snuck from her collection. I wanted Kai to have the full romance experience. Instead, she screwed up her face, told me to keep that washcloth away from her and ran, thighs clenched to the bathroom, just like now.

"Why are you smiling like that?" she grumbles at me, arms crossed at the foot of the bed.

Ah, she's back. Any whiff of vulnerability and Kaia's claws will come out.

"Just remembering. Come here, I want to hold you a little more."

She lets out a huff, but does as I say, climbing up with very little grace, then flopping down on her side. As soon as she's still I pull her into my arms, tucking her head under my chin. She's stiff for a split second, then melts into me, one arm tucked against me, the other thrown over my waist. Her lips press a soft kiss to the base of my throat and I know that I can't let this woman go. Not again. She's my heart, my soul, and I've not felt peace like this since she left without a word when we were eighteen years old.

"There are things you should know," she starts, and I know there are. I've felt it. But I'm also a coward.

"Shhh, baby. We have plenty of time for that. Let's just lie here and be with each other."

She nods, her curls catching in my beard. I brush her hair back out of her face, pressing my lips to the top of her head.

"You're mine, Kai," I whisper into her hair.

"Yeah, I think I am."

I wake when I feel rummaging in the bed. "Mm, what's going on?" After another two rounds with Kaia, I'm exhausted. Depleted. Especially after she sucked my soul right out of my balls that third time.

"Get up, lazy bones. We got kids to pick up." Something rough lands on my face, and I don't have to open my eyes to know it's my jeans.

Groaning, I roll up to sit, rubbing my hands over my face while Kaia laughs. "The joys of having kids buddy."

"I'm sure mom and dad will be happy to keep them a little longer," I grumble, looking for my shirt.

"I'm sure they could, but you're the dad and they're your kids so you gotta look after 'em. Come on, chop chop!" Kaia jokes but I know that she probably hasn't really spent much time away from the kids at all. An overnighter without them probably feels like she's missing a limb.

"OK, OK, I'm up."

I throw my clothes on, tucking my half mast dick into my pants. It doesn't seem to matter how many times I cum inside Kaia, he just keeps wanting more. I make my way out of the bedroom, freezing momentarily when she grins at me from the doorway. She's so fucking beautiful, and she's mine. She crosses her eyes and pokes her tongue at me, then squeals when I slap her ass, hurrying her out the door.

"Well well well, what do we have here? Is this big lump harassing you?" Pops teases from a camp chair he's set up directly outside the trailer.

"Dunno, Sid, looks like two happy younguns to me," Mad Dog adds from his matching chair, sunglasses covering his eyes.

"Is there a reason you boys are hanging around out here?" Kaia asks.

"Nope," Pops grins, leaning his head back, eyes closed. "Just taking in the rays."

Placing my hand on Kaia's lower back we move past the old boys. Mad Dog gives me a grin and a thumbs up, while Pops flips me the bird. I feel the overwhelming urge to tip his chair over, with his old ass in it, but as annoying as he is, he helped get me out of my head, and bring Kaia and I closer together.

Kaia grins up at me and for the first time in a long time, I feel at total peace.

Kaia

"You two better be ready otherwise I'll be leaving your asses behind!" I growl low so only the twins can hear me.

They're meant to be done with their chores at the diner, which only consists of them rolling the cutlery into napkins, but instead of doing their job, they've been slacking. Jax talking to some girls his age, and Annie sending glares to Chelsea Master's ginger kid.

"We'll be done in a minute!" Annie says, not taking her gaze off that Liam kid.

I roll my eyes and send Leo a message that we'll be running a little late. I'm sure he won't mind. The DRMC party is bound to run late anyway, given that tonight is the night that the Landrys, Gus and Jules are meant to be getting their cuts. It'll also be the night that Leo and I tell the kids that we are dating. I guess that's what we're calling it. I'm not actually too sure what we are calling this. He calls me his, and I guess in some way I always have been. Thinking back I don't think I've ever had this level of connection, both sexually, and emotionally with anyone.

"Hello, Kaia."

I freeze in place, my stomach dropping. No, it can't be. He isn't meant to be out for another two years. The courts would have told me, someone would have told me.

"Aren't you going to look at me, you little bitch? Thought I wouldn't find you? Well, guess again."

My eyes dart toward the kids who are blissfully unaware the fucker is here, in *our* diner. Turning slowly, I'm met with the black soulless eyes of the man who ruined my family.

"Seth."

"You owe me six fucking years, and I *will* get them out of you. Either in money, or flesh. Yours or Annie's, doesn't matter." He licks my earlobe and a shudder runs through my body.

It takes all my strength not to vomit in my mouth, but I manage it. He leans even closer and my hand strikes, gripping his balls as hard as I can and twisting my wrist.

"You come anywhere near my kids and I will fucking gut you. You hear me? I. Will. Gut. You. I'm not that weak, sad woman you turned me into anymore. I have fucking claws and I'm not afraid to use them." I hold his eye contact, watching as his face turns from red to a dangerous blue tinge from where I've stolen his breath from my hold on him.

I wait until his eyes start to roll back before I shove him away from me, releasing his balls as he crumples to the floor. Luckily I'm standing behind the counter, so my customers are none the wiser.

"You'll fucking pay for that, you bitch," he snarls, retching as he grips his balls protectively.

Annie spins in her seat and gives me a thumbs up, letting me know she and her brother are ready to go, finally. I smile and tip my head toward the door. Once I see her and her brother are out of the diner safely, I squat next to the man at my feet.

"Bring it on, you piece of shit. I'll be waiting." With that I turn on my heel, leaving through the back door.

"Come on, Mom. Weren't you the one waiting on us?" Jax

says with a smirk.

"Yeah yeah, just get in," I tease, all the while mindful to check over my shoulder. I can't believe my past found us. All I know is that history is not going to repeat itself.

* * *

"Yo, you OK, Little Mama?" Leo asks, pulling me into his side. He presses a kiss to my head and I soak up his warmth.

"I'm OK, just had a day, is all." My eyes meet my son's across the dancefloor that the DRMC has set up for the celebration. Jax's gaze moves to Leo, then back to mine and then he's moving. Beelining through the dancing couples.

He comes to the stop in front of us, looking from me to Leo. As if joined by ESP alone, Annie pops up out of nowhere to take her place next to her brother.

"Oh, is this what I think it is?" Her eyes are wide, and I can tell by her little shimmy that she wants to clap her hands for us. Not for the first time I realize that she's probably going to grow up to be a Mira-type person. Full of glitter and sparkles and excitement and joy.

Leo glances down at me, then back to the kids. "I've been meaning to ask you both, would you give me permission to date your mom?"

Annie turns to look at her brother, the two of them doing that twin thing they so often do. They hold each other's gaze for a beat, before they turn back to us. Jax steps forward, holding out his hand. Leo grips it immediately, pulling Jax in for a hug, then Annie.

"Thank you, I promise I'll take care of her." Leo whispers loud enough for me to hear.

He holds the twins for a long time, before scooping me up in his embrace, all of us sheltered from the world by Leo. It's perfect and wonderful and overwhelming in how right it feels, and with Seth coming back into my life I need to find a way to make sure I don't ruin this. I can't lose what we're building here.

"I'm just gonna pop to the bathroom, I'll be back." I press a kiss to the underside of Leo's jaw, then a kiss to both of my kids before wandering off.

I need air, to feel less suffocated by my past choices. I need to plan, I need to figure out a way to get Seth out of our lives for good.

"What are you doing all the way out here?"

I spin, startled by the gruff voice. I take a look around, not actually sure where "here" is until I spot the barn-like structure that we call the Rev Room now. I know this place well. This is where I saw the full extent of what it means to be part of the DRMC. Watching Chewy take care of Renae Sullivan, that was when I knew that no matter what, this place would keep my kids safe.

"Oh, just needed a little space. So I took a walk." I shrug, looking into the dimming light at Sniper.

I've been around the brothers long enough to know them all now. Some, like Rider and Flack and Tav are very easy to get along with. Others, like Sniper, are a little quieter, preferring their own company. Or in his case, the company of the brother he's been keeping alive.

"What are you doing all the way out here?" I return the question.

"I don't actually know," he answers quietly.

I blink once, then twice. I'm not sure if that's an invitation for me to ask what's bugging him, or for me to leave the man alone.

"You ever just wish you could let things go? Just get over it?"

"Oh, I'm the wrong person to be asking, buddy. Have you not seen me hold a mean grudge at Judge this whole time?" I smirk.

He stares at me, as if staring right through me. "That's not a real grudge. I know you want to be close to him. You'll forgive him, you know? You're already there. I, on the other hand, can't forgive."

I swallow, not wanting to concentrate on my feelings for Leo. "Can you forget maybe?"

"Not while he's still alive," His gaze moves to the Rev Room, as if able to stare right through the walls to his brother.

"Have you thought about ending it for him?" I inch closer, wanting to see his face when he answers.

"I don't think I'm strong enough." His shoulders slump and he stares at the ground. He takes a deep breath and then shakes his shoulders out. "We should get back, care to walk together?"

"Nah," I swallow, "You go on. I think I'll walk and think a little more."

He tips his head at me, ambling back toward the party, DJ Rider playing Shaboozy. I turn to look at the building behind me, Sniper's words ringing in my ears. He's a good man. Hell, the whole MC seems to be filled with good men. Well, kinda. I mean, they seem to kill people pretty well, but I don't think it counts if you're only killing bad guys. Probably.

My curiosity gets the better of me and I slip inside, the LED overhead lights flickering on. My gaze roams the large open room, settling on the man in the corner. I thought he looked terrible the first time I saw him, but now, he looks barely alive. He's covered in cuts and bruises, congealed blood. Aside from looking beaten to within an inch of his life, he seems to have all his body parts, so amputation wasn't one of the torture methods used on him. Although I can't imagine Sniper to be that kind of guy. I know a little about his background, Leo told me and I can see why he wants his brother to suffer like his sister did, however I also know that Sniper can't take this man's life.

Moving closer to him I spy the syringe on the stainless steel table. I've seen how Pops used it on Renae Sullivan, the woman who was selling babies, including her own. He gave her just enough to relax her before we essentially blew her up. There is more liquid in this syringe than the one he gave her, so I know this will work. My steady footsteps creep closer to the man, lying curled into a ball, whining like a pitiful animal. Removing the cap I hold it up so he can see it, and I'm surprised when his gaze fills with relief instead of fear.

"You know what happened to your sister, and instead of stopping it, you did it to other people's sisters, wives, girlfriends. You deserve everything your brother has done to you and more, but your existence is hurting him. That's why I'm doing this. Not out of kindness to you, but to your brother. Burn in hell." I stab the needle into neck, his main artery stark against the skin thanks to the lack of food he's been given during his time here.

I watch as his body slumps, his breathing slowing until there are no more breaths to take. Removing the syringe I replace the cap, throwing it in the sharps bin on my way out of the building, stopping when I come face to face with the man who has the same eyes as my children.

"You've done that before, haven't you?" Leo's bright green eyes stare into mine, searching for a lie.

"Yes, I have." I stare back, daring him to ask, daring him to just damn well ask what I've been through these past years.

We stand staring at each other for what feels like an eternity. His face doesn't give anything away. I expect him to walk away in disgust but instead he bands his arms around me, pulling me into his chest. "Kaia, baby, you talk, I'll listen."

Chapter 15

Judge

I didn't think she would do it. I thought perhaps she would see Sniper's piece of shit brother and take pity on him, help him, instead she did what Sniper couldn't bring himself to do. And she did it without flinching. In fact she didn't flinch until she saw me, one look at her and I knew she was about to run.

Looking around me I decide this is probably better done in one of the trailers, or better yet, the house I've built just down from Tank's. When Marx and Pops revealed there was space for us all to build cabins similar to Chewy's family, I leapt at the chance. Kaia's house is nice and all, but it's not near my family and more importantly, I don't live there. I want them here, with me, the way they should always have been. I take Kaia's hand, leading her away from the Rev Room, following the dirt track to where the houses are. I move past Marx's, Wire's and Tank's, coming to a stop in front of a cabin with a blue door and a wraparound porch. Guiding Kaia up the steps is enough to snap her out of her silence.

"Where are we?" she peeks inside the door when I swing it open, the inside bare save for two camp chairs where Tank and I had a beer last night.

"Welcome home, Kai,"

Her wide eyes snap to mine. "What?"

"I built this for us, our family. I want this Kai, you, me, the twins. Together, the way it should have been."

She sniffles, turning her back on me. "Leo, there are things you need to know. You might change your mind," her voice is small, her arms wrapped around her middle.

"I know that you've taken a life before."

She nods, looking so fucking tiny and vulnerable. "You need to understand, Leo, the me you know here, from the diner, that's not who I was for a long time. I never had many friends, I was insecure, and then I was a mom."

"Kai?"

She raises her hand, stopping me, "I need to get this out. Please?" I nod and she gives me a tight smile, before staring out the window, not looking at anything in particular. "I had a ... boyfriend. Seth. He was nice, charming. Was happy dating a single mom." she huffs, her voice detached like she's telling someone else's story. "We started off friends, then it slowly became more." She takes a breath, looking over at me. "I didn't realise how unhealthy the relationship was until it was too late. The barbs about my cooking, cleaning, my looks. Isolating me from my dad. Slowly chipping away at me until he controlled everything. The money, the house, the kids, me. I worked all the hours I could get and yet it was still never enough. Seth wanted me to earn more. Then one night he comes to me with an idea, to sell pictures of my feet. I mean, what could it hurt? No one would know it was me right? But that was just the start

161

of it."

My fists clench as my stomach sours. I don't want to hear it, and yet I need to.

"The next thing I knew it was live cam shows of my feet. Then the underwear I was wearing in the cam shows would be sent to subscribers. Then it was blurring my face out and posing for nudes. It all came to a head when I came home one night to find him and a friend waiting for me in their underwear, the camera pointed at the bed. I went nuts, knowing the kids were upstairs, knowing that Seth had arranged this without my knowledge. His 'friend' flipped out, told him to call him when I calmed down." She takes a deep breath, her gaze back out the window again. "He lunged toward me, slapping me so hard I saw stars. He was wild, threatening all sorts of things. Threatening that Annie would take my place if I didn't do as I was told. I freaked out, ran upstairs and locked myself in the twins' room." Fury rushes through my veins, the blood making my head pound with pure rage. "I couldn't let that happen so I called my dad to come get us then started packing. I woke the kids, told them we were going to stay with grandpa for a bit. They were so fucking excited. I waited the ten minutes it would take dad to get to us. I heard his voice shouting downstairs, banging, then quiet. Too quiet." Her shaking hand comes up to cover her sob, and I reach for her, stopping short when she swallows thickly, pulling her shoulders back. "I unlocked the door, snuck downstairs to see my dad lying on the floor, blood coming from his head. I ran to him, to help him and Seth, he-he grabbed me. I fought as hard as I could, I bit, kicked, scratched, everything I could think of but Seth was bigger, stronger. He slammed me into the wall, his hands around my throat, screaming how I'd cost him money. I must have blacked out because when I woke up Seth was on the ground, Annie was on the phone to first responders and Jax was staring at Seth with a baseball bat in his hands. My baby boy, my fucking baby had to save me from the bastard I had brought into their lives." She whirls to look at me, eyes wild, "That's the type of mother I am, Leo. A mother who brings a monster into our lives and whose babies had to save her."

I pull her into my arms, wrapping her tightly, rocking her side to side, "Shhh, baby, I got you. None of this is your fault. Men like that, they fucking choose women they can control. You were young, alone with two kids, an easy target." I push her away from me, holding my face in her hands. "When shit went bad you knew to get out of there. You're a fucking amazing mother Kai, don't let some fuckhead make you question your worth."

"But-"

"No buts baby."

"He's the reason Annie is skittish around men and why Jax is so overprotective." She cries again, staring at me as if I'm not taking her words in.

I'm hearing her loud and clear. I initially thought that was their personalities, but now I know what they all went through, the way they are together, it makes so much more sense. The kids are fourteen and yet they don't behave their age at all. Annie seems young for her age whereas Jax is like an old soul.

I hug Kaia to me tighter, silently trying to give her my strength. I know that she must be carrying a fuckton of guilt around what the kids went through, but shit, if they hadn't intervened, then she wouldn't be standing here right now and who the fuck knows what type of life the twins would have had living with that motherfucker.

I wait a moment until she settles, before murmuring into her hair, "What happened to your dad, baby?"

She swallows, her face pressed to my chest, arms wrapped around my waist. "They put him into a coma, but his brain never recovered fully. He came home with me needing round the clock care, feeding, changing, the works. He didn't want to live like that. Everytime I sat with him he'd use his energy to tell me to let him go, it wasn't the life he wanted." She sniffs, swallowing thickly, "So one night the kids and I had a movie night with him. We sat on his bed and shared stories and cuddles. Then once the kids fell asleep I held his hand and we said goodbye. I overdosed him on pain meds and lay with him. He pressed a kiss to my head and then he was gone."

I, too, press a kiss to her head and she breaks down, the trauma and pain and guilt leaving her body through her sobs and wails, my woman held together only by the safety of my arms. It breaks my fucking heart knowing what my family went through, but not for any longer. From this point forward every breath I take will be to make their lives better, no matter who I need to kill.

"Where is this Seth fucker now?" I growl as soon as she quiets.

"After dad died his assault and battery charge was upgraded to manslaughter. He went to prison, b-but he's out now. He found us at the diner."

A chill runs down my spine and I push her away from me, my grip on her shoulders tight, her skin under my palms the only thing keeping me grounded. "When?" I growl, ignoring her wide red rimmed eyes.

"Just before we left to come here," she whispers, shrinking in on herself.

"Fuck! Did he hurt you? Touch you at all?" I run my hands over her body, not fucking surprised that the bastard choked her out. She's goddamned tiny.

"No, he threatened me and Annie, but I-I grabbed him by the balls and twisted until he almost passed out," her lips tip up and I know that's a fucking big deal.

"Good girl," I praise, getting a smile from her before it fades.

Her eyes drop to her hands, "Do you think less of me? I put our kids in danger, I was selling myself, I-"

"Stop, Kai. None of this is your fault. Seth preyed on you, he targeted you and used you. *He* is the one who endangered our kids, not you. *You* are a fucking survivor. That bastard took your self esteem, your safety, your fucking father and yet you have survived and raised two amazing people. I am in *awe* of ,Kai. To the marrow of my bones."

She burrows into my much larger body and I hold her tight. "Now, tell me everything you know about this fucker. He's about to disappear."

Jax

"You know with Mom dating Da-Leo that school's gonna be even more shitty."

"Were you about to call Leo Dad?" Ugh, Fannie-Smella can be such a pain in the ass.

"No."

"Yes you were!" She grins then sighs. "I call him Dad and I think he likes it."

I nod. He does like it. He goes all soft looking. Which is weird cos the dude is massive and covered in tats.

"I like him, Jax. I want him to be our dad. Is that lame?"

"Nah, it's not lame to want a dad. Besides, he *is* our dad."

"And he seems like he'd be able to keep mom safe," Annie whispers, looking behind her. "He was there, at the diner, Jax. Seth."

My spine stiffens and I shake my head as the memory of the last time I saw that motherfucker comes to mind.

"Do you think Mom will move us? I don't want to leave the DRMC," Annie whispers.

"Why don't you worry about the kids at school and I'll make sure that fucker never comes near us or Mom again?"

"OK. I'm sure I can deal with the kids at school."

"What's going on at school?" Cove asks around the sucker in her mouth.

"Nothing," Annie says quickly, smiling at her and Jovie and Elio. "Just some kids giving me shi- um, crap, about being a DRMC kid."

Cove scoffs, rolling her eyes. "Kids are dicks. Want us to have a word?"

I stare down at the three of them. They're all about eight years old and go to elementary school. Well, Cove and Jovie do, Elio goes to a special school that Vi's sister teaches at. From the stories they sound like little shits.

"Ah, nah, you're all good. Thanks anyway," Annie says, trying not to laugh.

"Your loss," Cove shrugs, walking off with her gang.

"They're kinda scary," Annie says, and I nod in agreement, because, well, they kinda are. "You're gonna tell Dad, right?"

"Tell Dad what?"

Chapter 16

Judge

I impatiently listen through church waiting for Wire to finish his report on finances and some other shit I don't care about. Ever since Kaia told me her secret and Jax told me his plans, I've been quietly fuming. How dare some slimy fucker threaten my family?

"Good, thanks Wire. Anything else to add?" Marx looks around at each of us, holding eye contact for a moment.

I clear my throat and his surprised gaze finds mine. In the entire time I've been a brother in the DRMC never once have I had anything to bring to the table. "Ah yeah, so, Kaia told me something interesting last night."

"I fucking knew it! Knew she couldn't be as untroublesome as she seemed," Rider cackles, rubbing his hands together.

"Shut the fuck up Rider!" Marx growls, bringing his attention back to me.

"So, ah, shit." I sit, trying to find the right words, then throwing caution to the wind, "She ended your brother, Sniper. I watched her do it, she told him he was a piece of shit and she was doing you a kindness." My shocked brothers stare at me in silence, so, while I have a captive audience, I carry on. "She'd done that shit before, pumped an overdose into her father's veins after he was assaulted by her ex-boyfriend. Long story short, he was using her to cam girl, simple shit, feet, no face nudes, then she comes home one day and he surprises her with a friend and a camera."

"Motherfucker," someone growls and I damn well agree.

Running a hand down my face, I continue with the main points, "He threatens her that if she doesn't do it, he'll make Annie." A chair goes flying and Sniper paces, head back, looking at the ceiling, "She locks herself in with the kids, calls her dad, the ex assaults him and when she goes to check he chokes her the fuck out. She wakes up with Annie on the phone and Jax with a baseball bat in his hands and the scumbag on the ground."

"Fuck, brother," Tank's meaty hand lands on my shoulder, giving me his strength.

Marx takes a deep breath, blowing it out slowly. I can tell by the set of his jaw that he's pissed on my behalf. "How old were the twins?"

"Eight."

"Where is he now?" Sniper asks in a low, deathly calm tone.

"He was meant to be in prison but somehow got out early. He tracked them down to the diner, and threatened my woman and my baby girl." My hands fist at the thought that he had the balls to walk into her business to intimidate her.

"He dies." Sniper up and leaves the room, and the Pres lets him. Hell, the guy just found out that my woman ended the bane of his existence, I think it's only fair we cut the guy some slack.

"Those in favor of ridding the earth of this scum?" Marx asks, looking around at us.

Rider bangs his fist on the scarred table in the dining room, then Tank, followed one by one by my brothers.

"Wire, find out all you can about this –" Marx looks to me.

"Seth. Seth Carrick."

"On it, brother." Wire nods once, fingers flying over the keys.

"Judge, how do you want to do this?" Rhodie asks, most likely already planning strategies in his head.

"Don't care. As long as we get him before Jax does. His plan was to go after Carrick himself before he realized he doesn't need to do that shit anymore, DRMC will take care of it."

"Good boy you got there," Flack nods, "But kid needs to be a kid for a bit longer."

I tip my chin in agreement. That may have been how Kaia and the kids did shit in the past, but no more. They have a whole damn family at their backs now.

"Well, it turns out that Seth Carrick has a set of balls on him. Checked into a motorlodge just out of town under his own name and credit card."

"Dumb fuck," Savage snorts.

"Tombs," Marx looks toward Gus, Jules and Tav before doing a double take. "Where the fuck did Pops go?"

Looking around the table it takes a moment for all of us to clock that Pops somehow disappeared into thin air.

"He was here just a minute ago because he was bitching about Wire's report being too long," Dex smirks as Wire flips him the bird.

Marx runs a hand down his beard, "Fucks sake. Tombs, you're on Carrick surveillance. Landrys, 'you back them up. Mad Dog, TumTum and Chef, you're on Pops duty. I have a

169

feeling that fucker will go after Carrick himself if we're not careful."

Everyone nods and we all get up to leave once Marx bangs his fist on the wall behind him.

"Brother," Wire calls, stopping me in my tracks. "I'm sorry, I could have found out this shit if I had have dug deep-"

My hand lands on Wire's shoulder, stopping his sentence, "Wire, there's nothing to be sorry for. I wanted to hear *her* truth and I got it." I give him a little shake and he nods once, eyes back on his screen.

"I'll get the girls to help me. I'll go through everything we can to get any footage or images of Kaia taken down."

"Thanks brother," I manage to choke out.

I turn on my heel and head out to find my woman and the twins. After what happened yesterday with that Seth guy I decided to move them back into the trailer. I wanted to keep them near and I wasn't that interested in staying at their place. Here, we have the force of my brothers at my back if something was to happen. I would have moved them straight into the house I built for them and refused to let them leave, but even I know that two fold out chairs ain't comfy living.

I climb the two steps to the trailer door and let myself in. "Hey Dad," Annie grins at me. Jax gives me a chin lift and Kaia moves toward me, sliding in under my arm when I raise it.

"Hey, baby girl," I greet my daughter, before pressing a kiss to the top of Kaia's head.

I take in the scene around me and I've never felt such peace. Kaia urges me forward, her small body forcing me into a chair two times too small for me so I'm sitting at the tiny dining table.

"I'm making mac n cheese and Jax is on the steak," Annie

chats away busily.

Kaia joins me at the table, a soft smile on her face as she watches the kids. "How you doing, baby?" I murmur to her, the sound of the twins bickering in the background.

"Lighter. Scared. Ashamed." Her large eyes hold mine before she ducks her head. "Guilty." she whispers.

"Hey, hey, look at me," I pinch her chin in between my fingers and tip her face up to look at me. "We ain't doing that, baby, remember?"

She nods, sniffling before she pulls her shoulders back and gives me a tight smile. "Strong. I feel strong. And safe." She gives me a little smile and I feel about ten fucking feet tall.

"That's cos you are, baby."

The kids serve up dinner and we sit and eat. They tell me about school, although I can sense something ain't quite right there, Annie seems a little hesitant to share much, but I guess that's probably teenage girl stuff. Jax on the other hand is a lot more talkative than I've ever seen him, and I guess our chat earlier has probably helped with that.

"What are you going to tell Dad?" I ask, looking between the twins.

Annie eyes her brother, before staring up at me, worrying her lip.

We're in a standoff, and I know as the adult here I should be the one to broach the subject first. So I decide to lay it all out there.

"I know what you did, son. You saved your mom and your sister, and I'm so fucking proud of you."

His eyes widen and I don't miss the sheen in them as he looks away, nodding. I leave him to do whatever he needs to do, to recenter himself, so I wait, quietly, patiently, until he turns back to face me. He must read something in my face because he looks at his sister, then takes a breath, blowing it out.

"He's back. Seth. That's his name. Seth Carrick. I–" he gulps, "I was going to go after him." Annie gasps, frowning at her brother. "But I –I can't do it on my own," he mumbles. He looks at his hands, before looking back up at me. "Will you help me?"

I grab him by the back of the neck, pulling him into me. My other hand finds Annie and I draw her in too. "Of course, son, but leave it to me, yeah? You be a kid. Go to school, date some girls. Me and my brothers will take care of things, got me?"

He pulls back, looking sheepish that I've been hugging the shit outta him. "Yeah, I ah, I got you."

"Good. Now, shit, go off and have a good time! It's a party!"

Shaking off the memory I lean back in my chair, hand on Kai's thigh, laughing at my kids across the table. This. This is what I want every damn night, and I'm going to have it.

Kaia

"When were you going to tell us, hmm?" Chewy taps her foot as she leans against the counter.

The rest of the girl gang, including Pops and Mad Dog are lined up on the counter stools, staring at me.

"Ah, tell you what?" I ask, eyeing them all.

"About that dickhead ex of yours!" Blanche hisses over the top of her daughter's head in the front pack. I'm starting to doubt that child will ever learn to crawl or walk. She's always attached to her mom or her dad.

My eyes dart around the diner and I relax a little when I see that we're thankfully quiet. The only tables taken up are with school kids. Annie and Jax are sitting together doing homework, the big little kids are at a booth, scheming with some messy looking ginger kid their age, and there are a few booths with teenagers dotted around. One in particular made my baby girl shrink into herself when they walked in but Jax is with her, eyeballing Chelsea Wilson's kid and his crew who seem to be sneering at the twins. Little assholes.

Looking back at the girl gang, I close my eyes for a moment, then take them all in. "Look, I didn't want to-"

"Nope. No excuse, girl. You and those kids belong to us. You're in trouble, you tell us and we take care of it. That's how this shit works," Pops says, laying down the law.

My throat closes and my eyes start to burn knowing that all these people have my back.

"Hey, hey, now, none of that," Lovely coos, wiping a rogue tear from my cheek. "Look, it's quiet at the moment, why don't you take a seat and let us know how we can help you?"

I nod as she guides me to an empty seat in one of the larger booths, the girl gang, Pops and Mad Dog all cramming in with me in the center, like the meat in a crazy biker family sandwich.

Taking a deep breath I let it out shakily, "So, I'm guessing all your old men let you know what happened to us?" My eyes dart to theirs before looking away in embarrassment.

"We know what we need to know. If you want to tell us more, you can, if not, we're all good with that." Ana shrugs. "We just want his balls anyway."

"I just, I just feel so fucking ashamed," I moan, hiding my face in my hands.

"Why?" Chewy frowns, head tipped to the side as if I'm a mystery to solve.

"I let that man into our lives. I let him treat me like that, chipping away at me until even *I* couldn't recognize the person

173

looking back at me in the mirror. He made me weak," I end on a whisper.

"And? You're not anymore, and that's what matters," Chewy shrugs.

Lovely pats her on the shoulder, before turning to me. "Sometimes we are put in situations where the only way to survive is to appear weak. What do you think Seth would have done if you had fought back earlier?"

I sit silent, mulling over Lovely's words. Seth was charming, manipulative, and volatile. My mind flashes back to arguments where he'd throw things, the time he shoved me. He'd only gotten fully violent that one night, but that's not to say that he wouldn't have sooner if I hadn't bowed down.

"Ah, now she's getting it," Mad Dog says. "Sweetheart, chances are, if this version of you was in a relationship with Seth, he would have hurt you and the kids a lot sooner. Men like that, they crave control and feed off fear."

"They're the dangerous ones because they come across as good men," Lovely says, her voice strong. Her and Blanche know all about bad men masquerading as good men.

"They steal your light and that shit happens so slowly you don't even notice it. I was with Josh for months before I saw what he was like," Vi adds.

"Ugh, such a bland ham sandwich of a man," Pops says with disgust.

"He made me feel so small that I would do just about anything for him just so he would be proud of me. Sure Jules comes across as a grump, but that man works hard to show me how much he values me. It's not his natural setting to make a fool of himself, but he will salsa dance with me every chance he gets because he knows it makes me happy," Vi grins.

"Wire knew me long before we ever met in real life. He knew the real me. Knew what my life was like and even when he didn't know what I looked like, he'd send me messages and gifts to cheer me up. He games with me and wears couples costumes to Armageddon. He helps bring light to my life, he doesn't steal it." Remy adds, a soft smile on her face.

"Rhodie does too. He is the person who makes me better," Chewy adds, with a nod, no fluff.

Looking around at my friends, my new family, I voice the words I had been hiding from myself. "Leo is my light. He always has been."

"And you're his," Pops places a hand on my leg and gives it a pat.

"Soooo, can we now talk about what we want to do about this Seth guy?" Chewy asks and I throw my head back and laugh, blowing away all the seriousness.

"What the fuck is that?!" is yelled out and I spin to find Chelsea Wilson's kid pointing at the TV on the wall, a dangerous shade of red.

"Haha! Are you crying there? What a pussy!" The red headed kid sitting with Elio, Cove and Jovie yells with a mouth full of food. "Dude, aren't you like fourteen or something? I bet you sleep on a waterproof mattress," the kid chortles, as Toby Wilson, the fat bully gapes at the TV.

His friends all jeer, because why wouldn't they? They're all goddamn awful too.

"What in the hell is going on?" Nat mumbles, eyes glued to the screen as we watch tubby Toby dance around in his bedroom in his underwear.

"Turn it off!" he screeches, rushing toward the diner TV but freezing in his tracks when Jax stands, arms crossed, feet planted.

"You ain't turning shit off," he growls, reminding me so much of his father.

"Hey! What the hell!?" A kid from Toby's table shoots up, staring in horror at himself, crying on the big screen, begging some girl to go out with him.

The red-headed kid at Jovie and Cove's table roars with laughter, tossing a fry at the guy, "Dude, that is not how you get women. Even *I* know that and I'm only ten!" he gets dangerously close to rolling out of the booth because he's laughing so hard, and that's when I see it.

The remote to the TV tucked beside Elio, his fingers flying over his tablet. He taps something then his eyes fly to the TV just as the scene changes to another of the teens at Toby's table.

"Those little shits," Blanche mutters under her breath.

I stare back at the scene playing out. The havoc being caused by what's playing on the TV. Annie and Jax are roaring with laughter as are a couple of other diners dotted around. The kids who have been up on the big screen in less than a flattering light are arguing with each other as well as threatening legal action from their parents if this doesn't get taken down. It's chaos caused by three, no four, counting the ginger, little kids.

"How old are the big littles again?" I ask the girl gang, eyes wide.

"Technically eight, but morally at least twenty five with trauma," Mad Dog answers, watching the kids with a grin.

"Ah, should we stop this?" I ask, as I watch yet another teen have a breakdown in my diner.

"Nah, I have a feeling those little assholes deserve it," Blanche says. Then remembers she's the mother of two of the kids causing chaos. "I'll make sure Tav has a word with them later."

"I'm not having a word with Jovie, those kids are bullies. It's about time someone gave them a dose of their own medicine." Remy says, fascinated by the images on the screen and the now bully teens looking damned embarrassed, shrinking into the booth seats, some faces tear streaked.

The big littles pack up their stuff, and move toward us, Elio hanging back. He stands at the end of Toby Wilson's booth, staring for a long while. Long enough to make the older kids squirm.

"What the hell are you looking at?" one of the teens growls, but Elio doesn't flinch. He doesn't even blink.

He turns to look at Annie, before returning his gaze to Toby, staring as if Toby is a bug to squish. "I already decided what I'll do if you don't stop. " His lips tip up, a slow smile spreading across his face.

Toby must see something in Elio's face, because he swallows, then gets up, his gang of friends following behind him. They move through the diner, avoiding eye contact with Annie as they walk past her and Jax's booth on the way out, passing Leo, Tank, Rhodie, Tav and the three Landry brothers on the way in.

Leo takes one look at my face, then a quick look around the diner. "Ah, what did we miss?"

"Oh nothing, only that it looks like I'll be getting the big littles to help with my little problem," I smirk as everyone in the diner bursts into laughter.

Chapter 17

Judge

"**D**id you ban Jovie and Elio from using your laptop yet?" Wire gives me a look and I chuckle as I walk past him, taking my place in Church. I chuckle again as I think back to dinner last night, Kai and the kids pissing themselves with laughter over what the big littles did to Toby and his friends. Fucker deserved it if you ask me.

"We gonna have a problem with them?" Marx asks, looking around the table, gaze landing on Tav.

Tav shrugs, "Depends. If we try to stop them, we'll end up on their shit list. Wouldn't it be better to nurture their, ah, talents?"

Looks of horror fly around the table, and I can't help but sit back, arms crossed, feeling smug. My kids are fucking angels.

Marx squints his eyes, looking around the table with a frown. "Where's Sniper?"

Looking around, we all shake our heads, except for Pops who put on a real show of shrugging dramatically. Sniper has been struggling ever since his brother showed up. He seemed to shake off whatever was weighing him down when Kaia put his brother down, but he's still not himself. Anyone with eyes can see the man is barely holding it together.

"I'll catch up with him once Church ends," Rhodie murmurs. He's probably the closest to Sniper, and even then he isn't super close.

The curse of being a sniper means long periods of time on your own, isolation, silence. I'm not sure whether my brother Sniper was always solitary or if the job made him this way. Marx nods his thanks and clears his throat.

"Well, now is probably the best time to get this shit outta the way." He looks around the table at us. "As you know Moss Davies has recently been placed in the sheriff role. That means fucking good things for us." Everyone's fists bang the table in agreement. "But, shit aint gonna be all smooth sailing and a fucking bed of roses. There are snakes in the PD who worked for our dearly departed sheriff and are happy to be on the take, no matter who's paying." I nod, following along. Marx will have a plan, the question is, who will it affect? "Moss is looking for men to have his back." His gaze moves to Fox and Nitro. "You two are the only members who have a background in military law enforcement. How would you feel about giving up the garage, and taking on roles at the PD? Not as full time officers, because, I can't see you both being pen pushers and beating the streets, but just as backup for Moss as he cleans house?"

Fox and Nitro share a look, much like my twins do. They nod once, before turning back to Marx.

"He can have us for a year. No more," Nitro says, tapping his hand on the table.

"Moss will have you for as long as I say." Marx nods, Wire

179

tapping away at his laptop, probably putting that shit into the minutes. "Good. Second order of business. The Landrys, as with the Tombs, have done their time and are now fully patched. They're also ready to get home. Sniper has already put his hand up to transfer to the new chapter, help get it squared away. I'm opening it up for any brother who wishes to transfer."

We all share looks around the table. If I were younger and single I'd let it cross my mind. But as it stands, I have a family to think about.

"If you want an old fucker on your team, I'll throw my hat in the ring," Flack says, slapping a hand on the table.

"Flack?" Wire raises a brow.

"My baby girl is grown Wire, and she has you to take care of her." Wire nods, accepting Flack's decision. "Besides, you'll see me every time you lot get caught up in shit," Flack grins.

Chris snorts. Shit, not Chris, Saint. The Landrys finally got their roadnames and either we are fucking geniuses, or damned lazy. Each road name is a play on their government names. Chris is Saint, Victory is Vex, and Wisdom is now Omen. "So, every other week then?" Saint says dryly.

Our laughter rings out, only stopping when TumTum clears his throat. He shares a look with Chef, "I'd like to go, too. Seems like it'd be cool." Marx nods in his direction.

"Me too." Chef says in his low voice, earning a growl from Tav.

"Does my daughter know that you're thinking of up and leaving?"

"We've spoken about it. She ain't happy, but shit, I'm older than she is, she needs to live her life a little, without me holding her back," Chef frowns.

"Ah, another dumb shit," Pops mutters under his breath.

"Get back to me in a year or so kid, the Love Pres will sort you out," Marx and I laugh way too hard at his words. But hell, if anyone can sort out the clusterfuck Chef is going to get himself into, it'll be Pops.

"You find cover for the gym, I'll transfer." Our shocked gazes move to Dex. Of anyone I'd have thought he'd stay here, with Savage. "I ain't got a woman or a family. You'll need numbers to get shit moving in Louisiana. It makes sense to go."

Marx stares at Dex for long enough to make the brother squirm under his dark gaze. His eyes narrow, clearly scheming, before he nods in Dex's direction. "You sure about this?"

Savage slaps a hand on Dex's shoulder, giving him a shake. He looks gutted that his best friend and ex-VP is moving on, but shit, it's a good move. Dex will never progress to being part of the council here as we're so well established and he's not wrong, he ain't got nothing tying him to Texas.

"Yeah, I'm sure Pres."

Marx tips his chin, "It's settled then. It's going to be a fucking sad day for us, but having men I trust with my life and more importantly, with the lives of my family sitting not even four hours away, feels good."

"Never thought I'd see the day DRMC expanded past our little town limits," Mad Dog says, sounding choked up. "Fucking proud of you men."

We all nod, the gravity of the situation dawning on the faces of the Landrys and the men who are opting to move. It'll be weird without them, but having allies close by is a fucking bonus. Besides, if they grow as big as we have, DRMC will be a force to be reckoned with.

"OK, well that's that shit done. What have we got on this Seth Carrick slimy fuck?"

Banging in the hall has us all turning to look at the door. There's another bang and then it flies open, Sniper on the other side with a big fucker hogtied at his feet while Pops laughs and high fives him.

"Well, I guess we all know where Sniper was," Rider quips.

"It's a present for Kaia," Sniper grumbles.

"What a thoughtful gift." Saint says, eyeing the bruised and bloody man at Sniper's feet.

Marx lets out a sigh, "Right, lets get this shit over with."

"Want me to call the women?" Rhodie asks. Marx gives him a look and Rhodie snorts, pulling his phone out of his cut. "Chewy? Rally the girl gang."

Kaia

"Oh Kaiaaaaa, open uuuuuup!" Chewy yells from outside, before knocking incessantly at the trailer door.

Throwing the door open I'm met with not only Chewy, but the whole girl gang on my door step.

"Hey kids," Mira waves, "Do you mind helping Mama Debs, Sage and Niko with the little kids for a couple of hours?"

The twins share a look before getting up from where they're lounging on the couch to put on crocs and head out the door. But not before stopping to look at me.

"Go on, I'll be fine."

Jax raises a brow. "It's not you I'm worried about," he grins. Annie doing the same.

"What the hell?" I mutter. I hate when they do that. It's like they know something I don't know.

Before I can go down that rabbit hole Chewy reaches in and grabs my hand, before dropping it and wiping hers on the back of her pants. "Yuck I thought I knew you well enough to touch you but it grossed me out." She gives me a long look then turns and leaves.

I lean out my door, eyes following her before looking at the rest of my girls. "What was that about?"

"Dunno, but I heard Sniper has a gift for you," Blanche answers, waggling her brows.

"Yes! So let's get moving," Remy says, "To the Rev Room!" She lets out a giggle then follows Chewy, the rest filing after her.

Shoving my own feet into crocs I move to head out.

"Might want to wear closed toed shoes, girl," Pops says, staring at my crocs.

I eye him up then kick them off, opting for sneakers instead. "Perfect!" Lovely coos, twining her elbow through mine.

We walk in a loud, messy line from my trailer to the Rev Room, talking crap and giggling the whole way. Never in a million years did I see myself living this type of life. I have all these blessings thanks to Leo, and I think I owe it to him, to us, to try this thing. Properly. All in.

Walking through the door I'm stopped by Pops' long, low, whistle. "Damn, she's going to love it."

"I'm going to love what?" I make my way to the front of the girl gang only to stop in my tracks.

There, hog tied, bloody and bruised, is Seth Carrick. The asshole.

"Surprise," Sniper mumbles, looking awkward.

I gape from him, to Seth, then back to Sniper before launching myself at him, throwing my arms around his neck. Sniper stumbles back, surprised by my reaction.

"Thank you, Sniper," I whisper.

Leo's low growl reaches my ears but I ignore him. When you have a brother that does something so damn sweet, you need to thank him.

"You're welcome, little sister." He pushes me back gently, bending a little lower so his gaze holds mine. "You got rid of my monster, I'll help you get rid of yours."

"We all will. Now, where do we want to start?" Chewy asks, standing in front of floor to ceiling shelving filled with all manner of things.

Everyone turns to look at me. "Ah, can I help you?"

Leo chuckles, his large bulk moving behind me, bathing me in his warmth. His arm snakes around my middle as he leans down, "You're in charge, little mama. Tell them what you want to happen to this motherfucker." He presses a kiss to my temple before standing to his full height, not letting me go.

Seth's eyes are wide, darting between me, Leo and the rest of the DRMC. I can't help but look at him in disgust. I can't believe this asshole had me thinking so little of myself. I stare at him for long moments, thinking of all the things I want to do to him, the things I've seen Chewy and Pops do to men, and yet, I don't care enough about what happens to him in the immediate future. I only care what happens to him afterwards.

Raising my head I look at my friends, my family, all on tenterhooks on what my decision will be.

"I don't care what you do to him, I just don't want him to die."

"Huh?" Rider stops fiddling with some nunchucks made of dildos, to stare at me.

"You sure about this, Kai?" Leo murmurs softly.

"I'm sure. I want him to suffer. I want him to feel pain and fear and then when he's almost done I want someone, anyone, to disable him. I want him to live the life my father begged to leave. I want him shitting his pants. Incapable of caring for himself. I want him at the mercy of others."

"Damn girl, that's diabolical," Nat whispers, bumping me with her hip.

"Well, then, looks like we get to try some new techniques," Pops claps his hands, rubbing them together.

He and Chewy walk off to look at their supplies while I stand, warm and cosy in Leo's arms. We all watch on in silence as Pops and Chewy hold up all sorts of stuff and giggle amongst themselves.

"You said he made you foot cam, right?" Chewy calls out.

I nod once before ducking my head in embarrassment.

"No need to hide, babe, I for one think your feet are fucking adorable," Leo growls in my ear.

I can feel my face heat some, and Sniper smirks at me, having overheard Leo.

"He sold underwear too, huh girl?" Pops calls this time.

I can really feel myself flushing now. My whole body feels hot and it's equal amounts shame and anger. I break out of Leo's hold to rush up and kick Seth in the gut for what he made me do. Leo pulls me back against him, his scent and his warmth calming me slightly.

"Where did he sell them? Like online?" Mira asks, notepad at the ready.

"Um, yeah, a few sites," I mumble.

"So, you'd like wear them, and then just put them in an envelope?" She raises her brows, waiting for me to answer.

185

"Ah, no, he'd ah, vacuum seal them first."

Her eyes grow impossibly wide and it's almost as if the whole girl gang leans closer. "That's genius," she whispers.

The girl gang all share a look, before looking at me. Oh hell, they want me to help them sell their underwear.

"No one is selling panties!" Marx shouts, frowning down at his woman.

"Why not?" Chewy asks, head tilted, holding what appears to be metal underwear. Huh. Weird. "Sounds lucrative and people would pay good money for that. You could probably charge extra for wearing them to workout at the gym or something because they'd be more, what's the word? Flavorful? Anyway, it sounds like a great money making opportunity."

I nod along with her train of thought because she's right. It is a lucrative side hustle. "Worn underwear can be anywhere upwards of $30. Sweaty ones $80 and up."

All eyes stare at me and before I can shrink away I'm bombarded with questions. "Are there men's boxers on there or will I have to wear women's panties to make bank?" Rider shouts out, causing silence to descend. "What? We all need a side hustle in this economy."

"I repeat, no one is selling underwear from the fucking compound." Marx growls.

"What about from off compound?" Rider yelps as he jumps away from Marx's death glare.

"Now that we've agreed to start selling product to panty sniffers, can we get on with things now?" Chewy asks, blowtorch in hand.

I can't help the giggle that bursts out of me. The rollercoaster of emotions that comes with what we're about to do, with my ugly past dragged up and then somehow everyone now wanting to join the business I was ashamed of, all of it somehow breaks me down and puts me back together again. I beam at everyone in the Rev Room, hoping that my gratitude and love for them shines through my face.

I watch as Rider and Tank untie Seth and then hang him from the ceiling while Pops cuts off his clothing none too gently. Once he's standing in the nude, Pops' knife work clear to see, everyone shares grins. The show is about to begin.

Sniper bumps me with his elbow, a small smile on his face. "You good, little sis?"

"I will be."

Chapter 18

Judge

"You know, sometimes I watch Chewy and Pops and realize I'm not making the best use of my free will," Dex says, head cocked watching Chewy pour hot oil into some weird as fuck metal boots Pops strapped onto Seth's feet. Seth's blood curdling screams has excitement bubbling up in my gut eager to see what happens next.

"You got plans to use that free will?" I raise a brow at him.

"Heading to the new chapter I thought I might take a leaf out of Chewy's book," he replies, eyes on Pops using the smelling salts on Seth.

"You wanna become the icer?"

He swings his head toward me. "Fuck no! I meant, I might get a gator. You know, something to take care of."

Omen snorts, shaking his head at Dex's plans. "You do know that gators are dangerous, right? They'll take your hand off if you're not careful."

"Same as Chewy and Rhodie still loves her," Rider answers with a grin, ignoring Rhodie's growl.

"Babe, I need you to change the music," Chewy calls out ignoring Rider, "Now the feet are done I need something peppy for the junk," Chewy points at Seth's cock and balls, her nose screwed up.

"P-please no, n-no more, I swear, I swear that I'll leave and never come back," he sobs, snot and drool covering his chin as he wildly searches the room, "Kaia! Kaia! I'm so sorry, I promise I'll leave you alone, I p-promise!"

Kaia stands with a blank look on her face, staring at Seth like he's dog shit on the bottom of her shoe. She takes a step toward him, then another until she's right in front of him, head tipped back as she's at least a foot shorter than he is.

"You broke me, killed my father and threatened my kids. *My* daughter, you piece of shit. I hope you live a long, lonely, painful life." She grins at him, then takes a large step back, far enough away from him that my long reach can hook her by her belt loop on her jeans and drag her back into me.

"Proud of you, little mama."

"Thanks, baby," she murmurs back at me.

The LED lights that decorate the new Rev Room start pulsing to the opening beats of "You spin me right round" blasting through the speakers. Chewy claps her hands before spinning and shimmying over to Rhodie, leaning up to whisper in his ear.

"What do you think she's going to do now?" Kaia whispers over her shoulder, bopping her head to the music.

"I dunno. She mentioned his junk so it could be fish related." Tank says, staring at the matching grins Pops and Chewy sport.

"What the fuck are they doing with that cat food?" Switch yells, eyes wide.

"Oh oh! I know!" Mira raises her hand.

The girl gang including my fucking woman take off to find out what Mira knows. She starts drawing some weird as shit thing on a rolling whiteboard and the women all gasp before cackling.

"Tank, tell your woman not to leave her day job," Savage says, eyeing Mira's shitty drawing.

"What? No, she's an amazing artist. That's a, um, compost heap that she's drawing." Tank's head is cocked and he's squinting his eyes.

We follow his lead but I ain't seeing it.

"Baby, what's the picture of?" Tank calls out.

"Oh, it's his cock and balls," Mira grins.

"If that's what you're packing brother, I'd be seeing a doctor about it," Rider chortles.

"Yeah OK. Maybe she's a better writer than artist," Tank grumbles before winking at his ol lady.

Chewy and Pops have now not only covered Seth's privates with catfood, but they've also started to remove his boots.

"Switch, can you please stand by?"

Switch nods his head, stepping forward, eyes on what's about to be uncovered. Pops and Chewy share a look, then quickly release the catches on the metal boots and jump back, oil pouring out of them and down into the large drainage guttering in the floor. This version of the Rev Room is a shit ton more impressive than the one we used to have. It's around six times bigger to begin with, covered in sanitizable services and floor drains. Which kinda makes me wonder what the hell they were doing in here before they all joined the DRMC.

"Holy shit, it smells like pork belly!" Fox comments, staring at the mottled and burnt flesh of Seth's feet, some of his heel hanging off onto the floor.

"Yeah, I mean we pretty much deep fried his dogs," Chewy says as if it's an everyday occurrence.

"Third degree burn," Switch says in his booming voice, "at this level it's enough to destroy ligaments, muscle, fat." He waves at Seth's feet. The guy has been in and out of consciousness with the pain, but every time he blacks out, Pops hits him with the smelling salts and some form of "wakey wakey." "That's why it smells like that."

We all watch as Chewy waves Saint and Vex to get Seth down from the ceiling, then waves at them to lie him on the floor. She stares down at him for a moment, her fingers tapping their usual rhythm, before she leans forward, grabs his wrists then yanks him to the left, his dragging feet leaving skin and some type of meat in his wake.

"Argh, this shit is so messed up," Wire grumbles. "It's gross as hell but the smell is making me hungry."

"Oh! Mama Debs left snacks!" Ana announces, rushing away to one of the offices that come off the main Rev Room. In moments she's back, carrying a platter stacked with sliders.

"Oh nice, pulled pork," Rider snags two, stuffing one in his mouth like he's starving.

"You know," Omen Landry starts. "I grew up in a fucking evil place, right?" I nod, throwing my arm over my woman as she snuggles into me, handing me a slider. "I thought I'd seen all there was to see. But now I'm standing here with some of the best men and women I've ever met, eating pulled pork sliders, watching some guy have his feet deep fried with cat food on his junk." He takes a bite of his slider. "Fucking wild."

Kaia stares at him for a moment, before looking up at me with a huge grin. "He's not wrong," she takes a bite of her own slider, groaning around the tender, flavorsome meat.

"Babe, you gotta stop those moans," I murmur in her ear.

She stops mid chew, "Or what?" The little minx raises her brow.

"I throw you over my shoulder, take you to the trailer and fuck you all night. You'll miss knowing what happened to this piece of shit." I tip my head toward Seth, who yet again is snivelling and crying between passing out.

"Aw, you don't play fair," she whines, taking another bite and actively tries not to moan.

I snort at her, then press a kiss to the top of her curly crown.

"Rhodie, I need something super peppy babe. Tonight we celebrate the first time someone has been in the Rev Room and not gone out in a body bag. It's really unheard of and yet here we are," Chewy waves her hand around. She stares at the man at her feet, before squatting down, staring at him. "You better thank Kaia that she's willing to let you live," she pats his cheek hard, before shoving his face in Kaia's direction.

"T-thank you Kaia. I-I'm so sorry," he whispers through a throat that sounds raw as fuck from his screams.

"Thank me later," Kaia says, her gaze cold.

"OK, release the hounds!" Chewy shouts with glee as Pharrell's *Happy* comes piping through the speakers and Pops opens Chomper and Gretchen's playpen.

Kaia

"Do you think any of us need to be worried that Pops has in his possession chemicals that can pretty much turn you into a zombie?" I turn to Leo, trying to gauge the look on his face.

He stands on the trailer porch, his face screwed up. "I think it should be more worrying that Pops can even make that stuff."

I snort, nodding my head in agreement. After Chewy and Saint's gators ate Seth's junk, Pops injected him with some type of liquid that he assures me will render Seth pretty much in a vegetative state, but he'd be aware of everything happening to him. Kinda like that locked in syndrome I'd seen on Grey's Anatomy.

"Hey, you good with what we did tonight?" Leo asks, turning me toward him and tipping my head back so he can see my expression in the porch light.

"Hells yes! I don't want that fucker hurting anyone else."

"Well, he definitely aint gonna be doin that," Leo chuckles.

We watch as a blacked out town car comes slowly down the drive, pulling up near us, the motor still running. The passenger window rolls down, revealing Sasha's husband.

"Here for the package?" Leo calls out, friendly enough.

"*Da*, I have the perfect place for him."

"Where?" I call out, leaning around Leo who growls that I'm talking to another man. A gay one at that. Rolling my eyes I don't miss Roman's smirk at my behavior.

"Fiesty," he says, smirking at Leo. "Your *friend* will be housed at an asylum I happen to know is very reliable. I have many *friends* residing there as we speak." He gives me a warm grin which is completely at odds with what he's just implied.

"He's in the Rev Room with Chewy and Pops," Leo says, tipping his chin.

"Ah, the new Rev Room, I look forward to seeing it," Roman waves a hand as his window rolls up, the town car slowly making its way down the lane.

"I have no idea how he is Ana's best friend," I shake my head.

"Me neither, I'm just thankful he fucking is. Otherwise we'd never know where the hell to put a dickless, balless motherfucker to keep him alive until he dies of natural causes," Leo says, making me burst out with laughter.

He stares at me, his eyes roving my face at my laughter, my happiness. My giggles die down, only to be replaced by a gasp as Leo's lips smash into mine, stealing my breath. My eyes close of their own accord, my body melds into his and I groan when his large hands cup my ass drawing me into him until I can feel his thick cock between us.

He tears his mouth away, staring down at me. "Love seeing you happy, baby." He presses a kiss to that place near my ear that drives me wild.

"Leo," I whimper, my head rolling back as he drags his lips down my throat.

"Get the door, baby. I need you now," he growls, spinning me to face the door, nibbling at my neck.

My eyes are hazy as I try to concentrate on getting the key in the door, "Argh, why did I lock it behind me!" I whine, pushing my ass against Leo's erection, grinding against him.

"Open it now before I kick it in," Leo demands, rubbing his hard cock up and down my denim covered ass.

"Aha!" I yell triumphantly before I'm wrapped in Leo's arms as he carries me to the kitchen island.

"Hands on the island babe," I do as he says, the countertop cool under my palms.

Leo flicks the button on my jeans, yanking the tabs wide enough for the zip to slide down. He tugs them and my panties down my legs and I step out of them, kicking to the side.

"Fucking beautiful," Leo whispers, almost reverently, looking at my hail-damaged ass.

He jiggles the cheeks in his large hands before spreading me wide and licking me from clit to ass. I can hear him smacking his lips, alongside his groan as if I'm the tastiest morsel he's ever had. He raises one of my legs, resting my knee on one bar stool, then positions himself behind me. The thick mushroom head of his cock slides between my lower lips, spreading my cream through my folds.

"So fucking wet for me baby," Leo murmurs before his hips snap and he fills me in one long stroke.

I shudder at the intrusion, every fiber and nerve ending in my body coming alive as if I've been hit by lightning. Leo groans behind me, his hands gripping my waist and he moves me on and off his cock, thrusting harder, deeper each time until I can't feel where he begins and I end.

"You feel so good, Kai, so fucking good," he groans into my neck as he curls around my body, one hand dropping to circle my clit. "Like you were fucking made for me."

I pant in agreement, because I feel it too. Every curve of my body melds seamlessly with every hard plane of his, his cock filling me over and over to perfection, his labored breaths mixing with mine as I try to brace myself on the counter. It's all too much and yet not enough.

"Leo," I whine, pushing my hips back every time his snap forward.

"I've got you baby." I fly through the air as Leo lifts me, spins me around and then lowers me onto his cock, my arms grabbing onto his shoulders so as not to fall. "I've got you Kai, always," he whispers, slowing his thrusts, his arms banding around my waist, one fist in my hair, holding me close.

My forehead drops to his, staring into his green eyes, "I know Leo, and I've got you. Always." The words, those three little words are on my lips and instead of letting fear hold them in, I let them tumble into the space where our lips are pressed, touching, breathing, "I love you."

My words are his undoing, he holds me impossibly tighter as I bounce on his cock, his thrusts almost punishing as he fucks me with an urgency I didn't know I needed. My orgasm builds as my legs begin to clench around Leo, tighter and tighter until I arch back, stars bursting behind my eyes. I shake as wave after wave of Leo's cum fills me, his thrusts slowing but not stopping for another long moment.

"I love you, Leo, so much," I whisper, my hands cupping his handsome face, thumbs brushing against his dark beard.

"I love you, Kai. Always have, always will baby." he gently presses his lips to mine, sipping from them before pulling back.

I don't know how long we spend just staring at each other, but it feels right. Everything feels right. Leo. Me. The kids. The DRMC. All of it.

"Come on, little mama, let's get cleaned up and go get our babies." Leo pats me on the ass, then carries me to the bathroom.

"Our *big* babies," I say, because hell, they're almost adults.

"They're still our babies, no matter how big they are."

I nod in agreement, because Leo's right. They'll forever be my babies.

"Kai?"

"Hmm?"

"Have you thought about having any more babies? Shit, after what happened the last time, *can* you have more babies?"

I turn to look at him, his brows creased with worry as he reverently touches my stomach. Placing my hand over his, I smile gently up at him. "I can have more children."

"Um, do you want more?"

"You're a good father and a good man, Leo. My birth control implant will need to be renewed in a couple of months. If you, we, decide I could not renew and see what happens?"

His expression brightens, "Yeah, I like that. Don't get me wrong, I love my twins, but I kinda need you to be barefoot and knocked up so you'll never run from me again," he jokes, but I can still see the pain and guilt he carries for not being there.

Instead of telling him he's forgiven, I press my lips to his, telling him with my actions, my love. Pulling apart for air, I press a small kiss to the corner of his mouth. "The only running I'll be doing is to you, my love."

His grin is everything I need to know that this is where I'm meant to be.

Chapter 19

Judge

"We got everything?" I ask for the third time, because, well, these kids seem to just leave their shit all over the floor on game day.

"Yes, Dad," Annie rolls her eyes, slinging her backpack over her shoulder.

We all moved into our completed cabin two days ago, and it's been quite the crash course on living as a family. As a single man, an ex military one at that, I'm used to a small, tidy space. Now I have a home with people in it. More importantly, *teenagers* in it. Needless to say there's shit for miles.

"Everything is packed up and we're ready to go," Kaia says, wrapping her arms around one of mine. "Come on Papa Bear, let's go watch our babies kick ass!"

We all head out to the new SUV I bought Kaia and the kids. Yes she kicked up a fucking stink about it, but there is no way I was going to have my boy driven around in a damned matchbox car. Well, that and I could barely fit in the thing.

I wave out to my brothers who are lined up either on their

bikes or in the Tombs SUVs. It's game day today, and as with the last one, we have a DRMC pop up gazebo to set up along with the snacks and beer coolers. Even though it's only 10am. Removing my cut I fold it and hand it to Annie. It sits across her knees and she strokes the buttery soft leather, smiling at me when I wink at her. I love both the twins equally, but I would be lying if I said Annie didn't hold a special place in my heart. Her sunshine nature is exactly what grumpy fucks like me and Jax need in our lives.

Settling into the front seat, I give Jax a wink in the rear view, getting a chin lift back. I try not to smirk, but shit, the kid is a chip off the old block. I flash my lights at my brothers and slowly move down the drive. As Road Captain my duties don't stop just because I'm in a cage.

We arrive at the sports grounds and I snort when I see the other parents watching us through narrowed eyes. Kaia outright laughs and practically skips out of the SUV, waving at Chelsea Wilson and her blonde, bimbo BFFs.

"Do you think the girl gang will start another fight?" Jax asks, his hopeful face staring at me in the rear view.

I let out a sigh, "Look son, we can't wish for a cat fight every soccer game."

He rolls his eyes, before getting out of the car. A small hand pats my shoulder, "It's OK Dad. I'm sure the last fight was a one off."

I help Jax grab all our shit out of the back of the SUV and walk it all over to the gazebo Niko just finished putting up.

"*Tamariki*, what are the rules for today?" Mama Debs calls out, the big littles lined up in front of her.

"No gambling with juice boxes," Jovie diligently replies.

"And?"

Cove rolls her eyes. "And we're here to watch the game, and not get in trouble."

"Perfect," Mama Debs grins at them. "You can help me and your aunts with the babies."

"And if you're really well behaved," Switch begins, "you can help me with any injuries we come across." He grins down at them and I'm proud of the brother. Him asking to pull back his emergency room hours will be good for him. He was burning the candle at both ends and he really needs to slow down and enjoy the quiet time while we can.

"Yes! I hope there's blood!" Cove exclaims, grabbing Elio by the shoulder and shaking him in excitement.

"And bones!" Jovie adds.

Switch nods politely before turning to me and widening his eyes. I cover my snort. They're his problem now.

Wandering over to where my brothers are set up I stand and watch as the two sides get into position.

"You all ready for tonight, brother?" Tank murmurs, his eyes darting to his woman.

"All set. Kai's cut arrived yesterday."

"Glad it all worked out, brother. You deserve it," Marx says, slapping a hand on my shoulder.

Before I can swallow down my emotion, Pops and Mad Dog come to a stop next to me, "It seems to me the Love Pres has a 100% success rate."

Marx and I share a look. "I guess you do. Although, it would have worked out for Judge and Kaia with, or without you."

Pops slowly turns to stare at Marx. "Are you high kid?" Marx smirks and without a word turns on his heel and heads toward his woman and baby girl. "Little asshole. What the Love Pres giveth, the Love Pres can taketh away."

"Thats bullshit and we know it. Look how happy Lovely is, you know you can't take that away from her," Mad Dog says, looking ready to go to war for her. Those two are close. I think Mad Dog is the type of father Lovely deserves to have in her life.

"Yeah, alright." Pops eyes Marx and Lovely, "Doesn't mean I can't mess with him." Pops grins and shuffles off, hot footing it over to the big littles.

"Ah shit, who's in charge of him and those kids?"

"Debs," Me, Tank and Fox and Nitro say in unison.

"Thank fuck," Dex exhales.

The whistle blows and I watch as Jax runs up, lightly tapping the ball, his sister running in behind him in a practiced move. They're like magic on the field, their twin thing they do has them working in perfect unison.

"So fucking smooth the way they work together," Savage mutters.

Annie passes the ball to some dark-haired kid on the team but my eyes aren't on the journey of the ball. No, they're on that fat ginger fucker who's moving toward Annie.

"Take her out, Liam!" Booms across the field, Liam Wilson's fat fuck father has his fat fuck finger pointed directly at my baby girl.

I watch as his ginger kid turns to look at his red piggy dad, then at Annie. I see when he hesitates, I hear when his father yells the instruction out again and when Liam decides he has to do exactly what his piggy dad has said, his mother grinning widely.

"Oh hell no," I growl readying myself to step in between my baby and the ginger before I teach his fat fuck father a lesson.

Liam starts to pick up speed, headed directly for Annie like a heat seeking missile. Her eyes grow wide but before Liam can make contact Jax rams into him from the side, pushing him away from his sister.

Chelsea Wilson screeches from their side of the field, barking instructions and calling our women skanks and whores while her husband stomps over to our sons who are tussling on the muddy ground.

"Oh it's ON again!" Mira yells and all hell breaks loose.

"Wooo! I called it! Hand over my winnings, brothers," Rider shouts.

"They're just having words, no blows have been traded!" Savage yells back.

"Give it time!"

Kai goes flying across the field, meeting Chelsea Masters in the middle, the rest of the girl gang facing off with her cronies. I have no idea what Chelsea says to Kai, but I've seen that look before and it's not going to end well, I know that.

"Ow! You bitch!"

Our heads snap toward the sound, my eyes widening when I realize it was Lovely that struck the first blow, "Say that again, bitch!"

"Shit! Buttercup! Get away from that woman!" Marx legs it to his old lady while Rider, Rhodie and Chef demand payment from the brothers who bet that this shit wouldn't happen again this week.

"Get off me asshole!" Jax yells. He throws his elbow to shake Liam's pig face father off him, connecting with his piggy nose instead.

"You little fucker!"

"Don't. Fucking. Touch. My. Son." I grit out, Fuckface turning even more red than before.

"Tell your trash to keep his hands off my kid before I make a few calls to make sure he *never* has a future in this town," he sneers, blood dripping down his chin, looking at us like we're dog shit.

"Oh yeah?"

"Yeah."

With that one word I rear back and punch him directly into his doughy fucking face. The wimp collapses in a heap, a wet patch forming on his jeans.

"Pussy," Jax spits, staring down at him.

The ginger kid stares shocked eyes at his father, then at me, "I'm sorry, I shouldn't have. I should have just left her alone. I don't want any trouble," I follow his gaze to where it keeps flitting between me and something behind me.

Turning, I find Elio there, staring at Liam with a bored expression. "Do me a favor kid. Get a fucking hobby or sport you like and don't listen to your douche bag father, got me? You target my kid again and you'll have more than Elio to worry about."

Liam nods profusely and gets up, hurrying away to lick his wounds, leaving his father on the ground behind him.

"Huh. I just thought he was an asshole. Maybe he's an asshole because his parents are. I mean, he's shit at school and at sport, but it must be hard to be crap at everything with judgement dicks for parents," Jax says, watching Liam walk away.

"I'd say it's because he's a fat ginger," Rider says, looking smug with his winnings.

"As an ex-fat ginger, I agree with him. Ginger kids are the worst." Switch looks over his shoulder at the smart mouth ginger kid the big littles sometimes hang out with, and lets out an exaggerated shudder.

"So, who started it this time?" Moss Davies asks, coming to stop next to us, hand resting on his service weapon.

"Would you believe me if I said it was the other side?" Fox asks.

Moss gives him a bored look, "From one eye witness I've spoken to, it was Lovely who threw the first punch."

My brow raises, "Who did you speak to?"

Moss points to the ref, standing on the edge of the field. "Fucking snitch," Nitro mutters, heading in the ref's direction.

"Ah, shit," Moss moves quickly onto the field, just in time to catch Vi's swinging hand.

My brothers and I stand on the sidelines, watching the chaos. The kids soccer team have clearly chosen sides, cheering on the DRMC women. Vi and Moss are having an animated conversation in Spanish and the big littles seem to have gone back to their hustling ways.

"They're never having us back, are they?" Savage asks, watching the chaos.

"Nope," Tank replies, taking a long draw of his beer. Tapping me in the stomach with an unopened bottle in his hand, I take it, nodding at him.

"Thanks, brother."

"Anything for family."

Kaia

"Argh I can't believe those assholes banned my babies from the team."

"Does it help that Chelsea and her mean girl gang had their kids banned as well?" Leo asks, brows raised.

"I guess," I grumble, crossing my arms over my chest, pouting. "I just don't like that my babies aren't allowed to do something they love."

"It's OK, Mom, I can join the volleyball team or something, and Jax's huge ass should be playing football anyway," Annie grins at her brother who glares at her.

"Still, I don't like it."

"I know, baby. How's your cheek feeling?" Leo tries to distract me.

"I can't feel it thanks to the peas you put on it. And whatever that cream is that Mama Debs gave us." I scowl at the thought that I let that horrible mole get a slap in. On the upside I'm pretty sure that I broke her nose, so I guess we're even.

"Knock knock!" is sung from outside the front door before it's almost kicked in. "We're here to cheer you up!" Blanche says, swanning in, looking not quite right.

"OK, we'll leave you to your girls," Leo kisses the top of my head and hauls ass out of the house, the twins following behind. I asked Annie if she wanted to stay but apparently, like her brother, they would rather hang with the younger prospects and Sage than us. No worries, I will teach Annie the ways of 1997 Silversprings Stevie Nicks at a later date.

My girls all swan in, taking places on the couches or in Chewy's case, the floor.

"Why do you look weird?" Chewy says, staring at Blanche.

"Huh? I look the way I always do. Although I showered and got that grass stain off my face from soccer this morning."

"No, that's not it. Something isn't right." Chewy narrows her eyes at her sister-in-law, staring at her until it becomes uncomfortable for all of us.

"Wait, where's Tess?" I ask, sitting up slightly when I realize I don't think I've ever seen the woman's front before.

"Oh, she's with her daddy," Blanche smiles.

"That's it! That's why you look weird. I think you should look weird more often. It can't be healthy wobbling around with that baby strapped to you all the time," Chewy says matter of factly.

"Wobbling?" Blanche's brows rise higher and higher on her face.

"Anyway," Lovely claps, admirably changing the subject. "How are we going to get back at those awful women?"

"Who says we have to have anything more to do with them? All the kids have been kicked off the team, we'll never see them again." Vi shrugs.

"Ah, that's not true. They come into the diner every Wednesday for 'girly catch ups!'," I say in a high pitched valley girl voice.

"I agree with Lovely then, what are we going to do? We can't let this lie," Nat joins in.

"I could dox them online," Remy offers. I'm not sure what doxing is, but it sounds bad.

"Nope. We need public humiliation. Something so everyone will see how awful they are and they'll never show their faces in the diner again," Ana adds.

We all stare at each other. "Could we-?" I whisper.

"Yeah, but we have to do it classy. No dancing in their bedrooms in underwear. Leave it with me," Chewy says, staring into space, fingers tapping.

I have no idea what she has planned, but it'll be messy. I mean, those bitches picked on Chomper and if I know anything about Chewy, no one messes with her gator. Or her kid.

"So, we have like, three hours to go before the party tonight. Who wants to do extreme makeovers and surprise the men?" Mira asks, bouncing in her seat.

"I do!" Booms from outside the door and Pops and Mad Dog walk in. It seems the girl gang has grown by one more grandfather.

"Oh, what do you have in mind? Lose the Skechers?" Ana snickers.

"I'll have you know that these fuckers have the softest soles known to man. It's like walking on babies. That's how soft and squishy they are."

"Ew," Remy screws up her nose.

"It's a metaphor sweetheart. Or something." Pops waves his hand in the air. "Anyway, did I hear extreme makeovers?"

"Why yes, you did," I grin. "What do you suggest?" I wag my brows, expecting him and Mad Dog to run.

Instead, Mad Dog tilts his head, looking thoughtful. "Have you ever straightened your hair? I think that would change your look drastically."

I stared wide eyed at him as the girl gang, except for Chewy, gasp and then coo in excitement.

"He's right, you'd look soooo different!" Remy claps her hands in excitement.

"Oh oh, do me!" Mira waves her hand in the air.

This time Pops looks her up and down. "How about something biker chic? You always wear colorful dresses, how about all black, and those spray on black pants the ladies seem to like wearing?"

Mira's eyes grow so wide at the suggestion that I can't tell if she's shocked or offended. "Tank is going to DIE!" she squeals

207

so high pitched that only dogs would be able to hear it.

"What's going on?" Mama Debs pops her head inside the door that Pops left open, before coming in and snuggling into Pops' side.

"Pops and Mad Dog are giving us makeovers," Blanche says.

"Not me. Rhodie thinks I'm perfectly fine the way I am." Chewy nods decisively.

"Yes you are, baby," Mama Debs kisses Chewy on the top of her head, then smiles gently as Chewy beams at her.

It's not often I notice Chewy engaging in typical interactions, so to watch her with Mama Debs is something else.

"Mama Debs brings out the best in people," Lovely whispers, smiling in Mama Debs direction.

"Pity it didn't work for her own daughter. She's a total - ow!" Blanche hisses when Ana elbows her in the side. Hard.

"What was that you were saying my dear sweet sister-in-law?" Ana says, her voice sweet like honey.

Blanche narrows her eyes and flips the bird.

"So, are we doing this or not?"

* * *

Well, I can see when Pops and the ex DRMC Pres put their minds to something, they get stuff done. I'm standing in black skinny jeans and a pink off the shoulder top, with my curly hair now sleek and almost to my butt. Mira is in all black which looks all biker chick hot, but Mama Debs also curled her hair so she's looking like a curvy Sandy from Grease. Nat has her hair pulled back in a sleek ponytail, and she's wearing a dress which I've come to find out she never does. Same as Blanche, who somehow let Pops dye her hair. You heard that right, our resident raven haired mama is now a deep auburn and I can't believe how good she looks. Lovely stuck to her dark locks but is in a slinky red dress that Marx will swallow his tongue over. Remy is still a blonde but in leather pants and a kickass leather vest that makes her boobs look like they're staring you in the face. Vi's spray on pants really accentuate her hourglass figure, her hair poofed up looking all sexy like and Ana, who is the classiest of us all in her pencil skirts and silk blouses is standing there in a short as hell backless clubbing dress looking so hot that I'm seriously thinking of switching sides.

"Holy crap we look so good!" Lovely exclaims, and I know she means it because that woman never curses.

"So good. The party ain't gonna go for very long with us looking like this," Chewy says, her hair wild around her shoulders in a sparkly top, tight, ripped black jeans and her platform Doc Martens.

"You'd like that wouldn't you? Being thrown over Rhodie's shoulder caveman style so he can take you to his lair and have fun with you," Mira says teasingly.

"If he wasn't so big I'd do it to him first. I've tried picking him up but logistically it's a nightmare."

We all snort, I mean, no shit Sherlock. The man is at least a foot taller than her, and outweighs her by at least 80 pounds. It's admirable that Chewy even thought to try it.

"Wait, did you for real try to throw Rhodie over your shoulder?" Remy asks, wide eyed.

"Of course. What if he accidentally forgets to turn the gas off one day and I get home to find him passed out on the ground? It'll be up to me to get him over my shoulder and get him to safety," Chewy explains. Her gaze flits over us before her brows pinch. "Have you never tried to lift your men?"

"Ah, that would be a hard no, there Chewy," Blanche says.

"What if Tav was in trouble?"

"We're part of an MC. If Tav's in trouble one of his brothers will be right there with him," Blanche shrugs.

I mean, she has a point.

"Well, don't come crying to me when you can't save your men by carrying them from a gas filled building." Chewy rolls her eyes before straightening. "Let's go."

We all hop to attention and follow her out like a gaggle of geese, Mad Dog and Pops bringing up the rear.

"The men won't know what hit them!" Mira laughs excitedly as we all teeter on our heels.

For the first time in a long time not only do I have a wild group of friends, I have a family. I also have sleek hair and my cheeks hurt from smiling so much.

"Oh, before we get there, I got us all a little surprise to celebrate the new chapter. So, don't act surprised when it happens, just go with it." Chewy smiles then turns to fling open the door.

"Let's party!"

Chapter 20

Judge

L ooking around the scarred Church table I can't believe that tomorrow we'll be saying goodbye to some of our brothers.

"When the DRMC was first started, it was a place for vets to land, to get used to being back on US soil, and to adjust to a life we had left behind. Some of us had been in a bad way, but we all banded together in brotherhood. We've been through some shit together, and I can say this, from the bottom of my heart, that there are no better men I'd have at my back, than you all. This isn't the end, it's a new start. New brotherhood, new location, new allies. It's been an honor riding with you all. " Marx looks at each and every one of us gathered around the Tombs dining table, lingering on Sniper, Dex, Chef and TumTum who will all be leaving to ride with the Landrys in Louisiana. "As Pres of the mother chapter I'm appointing Dex as chapter President-"

"Fuck yeah!" Savage jumps up, throwing his arm over his original club brother, beating him on the back.

Marx waits for the rest of us to shout our congratulations before raising a hand, "Sniper, you're VP my friend." Celebration rings out again, Sniper tipping his chin at Marx. "Chef you're SAA, Omen Enforcer, TumTum Road Captain. Vex I want you as Chaplain. I know it may not sit well given your background, but as a brother you always lend an ear, are steady and have a fucking good sense of right and wrong."

A smile plays on Vex's lips, "I'd be honored, Pres. I may not live a religious life like I once did, but I have a spiritual and moral compass that I'd like to exercise."

Marx nods and not for the first time I thank my lucky stars Marx is my Pres. He may be rough and gruff, but the man sees shit in us that no one else does.

"Well, then, I'm calling church over. Let's fucking party!" Marx roars, thumping his fist against the wall. Shouts go up and I follow my brothers out, making sure to congratulate my brothers on the way out.

"What the fuuuuu-?" Rider's voice goes up at the end and we all stop on the deck, staring at the backyard of the clubhouse.

"Surprise!" the women all shout.

There's too much to look at. There's a fucking massive pool in the center of the yard with not only Chomper and Gretchen, but some type of grandaddy gator because this fucker has to be at least eight feet long. Not only that but he's wearing a tutu and a straw hat on a jaunty angle. There is some voodoo looking guy shaking a weird looking maraca at us, a bouncy castle shaped like a massive alligator, another weird looking guy making gator balloon animals and the women are dressed to the nines in the center of it all.

"Chewy!" Marx bellows and makes a move to step toward her but he's stopped by Rhodie's hand landing on his shoulder.

Rhodie slowly shakes his head at Marx, sighs and moves toward his Ol Lady.

"Surprise!" Chewy yells in her slightly monotone voice. "It's a gator themed party because the new chapter is in gator country." Chewy beams at her man and I take the opportunity to make my way to my own woman.

I've never seen her looking like this and while its sexy as fuck and my cock is a steel pipe in my jeans, she's not the Kaia I know and love. I love her big messy curls, her tight tops and jeans. This Kai I will have for the night, beaming at me looking all sexy with her sleek hair, but tomorrow morning I want my woman back. Sassy ass attitude and wild hair, all mussed from sleep or my hands running through it. Fuck. I need to get her out of this party and back to our cabin because I'm not sure how much longer I can stand my dick pressing up against my zipper.

"Hey, baby," Kaia grins up at me, her eyes dancing.

"Hey, little mama." Her brows pinch as she gives me the disapproving look she does when I call her that. Fucking adorable.

"Do you like what you see?" She holds her arms out and spins in a circle.

I have to hold back my groan when I see her ass in those tight black jeans. It's perfectly thick, round and juicy and I can't help but lash out and slap it on its way past.

"Hey!"

"Sorry baby, I'm just a man. I can't be expected to see that ass and not touch it." She rolls her eyes, giving me enough time to snag her belt buckle and pull her into me.

Tilting my head I slam my lips onto hers, her gentle moan all the permission I needed to slide my tongue into her mouth, tangling with hers. Tearing my lips away, I run my fingers up the back of her neck, gripping the strands in my hand at the back of her head.

"Fuck baby, I can't wait, need you now."

She gazes around, then gripping my hand tugs me behind her until we're out of earshot of the party and pressed up against the far wall of the clubhouse. I pin her to the wall with my bulk, my hand on her cheek as I tip her head back, demanding her mouth. Our tongues duel, building up urgency as our bodies rub and collide with each other. I tear my lips away and before I can command her to lose the jeans, my woman is already tearing at the button, rolling them down and stepping one foot out, her jeans and panties tangled around her other leg.

Unzipping my jeans my cock kicks as the warm air hits him, jutting out of the front of my jeans. Kaia licks her lips and I go wild. Gripping her under her plump ass I lift her high enough to line my cock up with her dripping cunt, surging inside her. I groan into her neck as her pussy grips me. Pressing her into the wall with my chest, I pin her there as I surge in and out, snapping my hips at just the right angle to have her eyes roll back. Her gasps and whimpers drive me wild and I don't think I'll last much longer.

"Fuck Leo, just like that baby, don't stop, don't you dare stop," Kai whines, her long, sleek hair shining in the last of the daylight, her dark eyes blown, lips parted.

"You feel so good, baby, but I need you to come. I need you to cream all over my cock," I grit out as I power into her on the angle she begged me for, bouncing her on my cock.

"Hmmmm baby, oh my god yes!" Kaia pants, her hips gyrate to the same rhythm I've set, her hard little nub rubbing against my pelvis as I grind into her. "Please Leo, please!"

I double my efforts, fucking harder, deeper, Kaia's heels bouncing off my ass as her short legs wrap around me. The tingle in the base of my spine starts and my balls draw up just as Kai's body stiffens and she throws her head back, jerking as if she's touched a live wire. I grip the back of her head, tucking my face into her neck as we stand, still connected against the wall.

"Oh my god, Leo. That was too much, too good, too-" She waves a hand around before letting it drop limply. "Too much everything," she sighs in contentment.

"I know baby, I felt it too."

"Do you think it'll always be like that?" Kaia asks, unhooking her legs from around my waist.

"Of course. You're you, I'm me, and this is how we make love."

She raises a brow at me.

"What? We may like it hard and a little rough, but we never fuck. We make love. Every. Single. Time." I punctuate the words with a kiss on her red, kiss swollen lips.

She smiles shyly up at me, then screws up her nose when she realizes she has my cum leaking out of her pussy.

"Let me help with that," I smirk as I press two fingers into her wet hole, pushing my seed into her for safe keeping. "There baby, now put your panties on and let's head back to the bonkers party."

She rolls her eyes and I'm sure she calls me a "caveman" under her breath. I don't care what she calls me, as long as it's hers.

Holding my hand out for hers, I twine our fingers and swing them between us as we head back to the party. Marx looks marginally calmer, and I guess the entertainment is staying.

Could be worse. Could be police strippers.

"What's with the gators?" I ask Kaia as we stand at the end of the party, watching.

Mira and Tank are dancing. Tav, Blanche, Jules and Vi are all in conversation with Vi's sisters Lily and Jazz. Nat and Savage are with Dex before he leaves for Louisiana. Remy and Wire are snuggled up and Rhodie and Chewy are showing Rider how to put a leash on the giant gator in the tutu. The rest of my brothers are milling about, enjoying the company. Shit, even Roman, Sasha, Dima and Moss have turned up.

"Oh, Chewy wanted to celebrate the new chapter," she says, like that explains everything. I stare at her until she rolls her eyes, then waves toward all the alligators. "They're from the swamp? Like the new chapter?"

Looking at the paddling pool set up and the various gators I can kinda see what the plan was.

"That doesn't explain the weird voodoo guy," I point at the guy who clearly isn't any type of voodoo anything. For one thing he looks like an elderly priest that got into the face paints, and even I know that voodoo practitioners don't go to parties as entertainment. As if to drive home my point he shakes his maraca at Rider.

"Your karma is terribly off," he starts in a creepy, breathy voice before throwing chicken bones at Rider's feet.

"Hey! What the hell man?" Rider shouts, kicking the bones away.

"Halt! Your aura is unclean due to too much self love! I have to cleanse you!" The bayou witch or voodoo doctor or whatever the fuck he is walks right up to Rider and hits him in the face with one of those smudge stick things. Rider sneezes into it, blowing ash and black sooty shit into his face.

"Excuse me, I'm looking for Sidney Tombs?" A pretty, dark skinned woman asks, stepping into the backyard.

We all stare at her as she stares at Rider who looks like he's in total blackface, the only thing showing are the white's of his eyes and his teeth.

"Ah, do you mind telling us who you are and why you are looking for Sidney?" Mama Debs asks, full of sugar but you can hear the steel thread to her tone.

"Oh, yes, sorry ma'am, my name is Zadie Jameson, and I've been asked by Happy Glades Retirement Village to pop by and run a welfare check. We've heard that Sidney is an elderly gentleman interested in our care," She smiles gently.

"What the fuck?! I don't know where you got your information sweetheart, but I'm not elderly-" he glares around at us when someone snorts, "- and I'm not interested in any old people home. Who called you?"

Zadie chews on her lip, opening her cellphone and tapping the screen a few times, "Hmm, there's no name, but they've put down they're a concerned member of the public because they believe you are a danger to yourself. It says here you have access to a motorcycle, which is not ideal for your season of life. Also that you may possibly have dementia."

"*Dementia*? Are you fucking mad!?" Pops is spitting.

"I'm so sorry, sir, it's just the notes state that you sometimes have crazy notions. It says there are often loud noises coming from this property, and sometimes you refer to yourself as," she looks down at her notes, "The Love Pres? Referring to yourself as a character is sometimes a sign of dementia."

Pops looks like he's about to shit himself at the thought that the tiny, sweet voiced woman will take him away at any moment. His eyes are wild, darting around, looking for an

217

escape. I can clock the exact moment he realizes that he'll never be able to outrun the sweet woman in front of him, so he changes tact and puts on the charming old man act.

"Look, love, I know you're just doing your job," he starts off softly, earning a smile for his efforts, "but I am of sound mind and perfectly fine. Please tell your boss that I will not be needing your services." Before she can say anything in reply, he shoves Chef her way and hot foots it as fast as his Skechers can take him. "No fucker is taking me to hang out with people who shit their pants!" He yells over his shoulder, making it as far as the large bush at the side of the clubhouse. We all watch as he disappears to a crouch behind it.

"Ah, I have a sedative and some colleagues that can help wrangle him if need be," Zadie starts, staring at the same spot we all are.

"Fuck off with your goons! You'll never take me!"

"Love, look, you seem like a nice lady and all, but Sidney Tombs is of completely sound mind." Gus says, almost convincingly. "I have no idea where you got your information, but trust me when I say that my grandfather is safe with us and he will behave from now on. Right?" Gus yells over his shoulder.

"Maybe," Pops yells back. None of us miss his grumbling and calling us assholes from his spot in the bushes.

"Here, why don't you let me show you out?" Rider smiles, the white of his teeth stark against the soot of the smudge stick. She stares at him in horror but follows him anyway.

As soon as she's out of earshot Pops emerges with leaves in his usually impeccable white hair. Snickers can be heard but none of us are brave enough to laugh out loud. He'll probably poison us or something shit..

Pops makes his way back to the party before he turns on us,

voice low, "Which one of you assholes set me up?" He hits us all, one by one with this narrowed gaze. "Come on, if you fess up now I promise there will be no retribution," he continues trying to coax us, staring until his eyes widen when his gaze lands on Kaia. "It was you, wasn't it? I *knew* you were planning something after the whole chilli episode."

Kaia smiles sweetly and Pops twists his lips, nodding before holding out his hand. "Well played, girl. Well played."

Kai takes his hand then pulls him in for a hug, whispering something in his ear. He barks out a laugh, pulling back with a smile on his face. "Lets you and I have a talk, huh?"

"Well, that took an unexpected turn," Rider mumbles, stepping up beside me.

"Brother, do something about your face," I shake my head, eyes on Fox, Nitro and Jazz. Huh. That's interesting.

"What? Do I have something on it?"

I slowly turn to look at Rider looking confused. "Um, might wanna check in the mirror brother,"

"As long as it's nothing too bad. That Zadie woman was hot as hell," he mumbles, heading off into the house.

"Have I told you lately how much I love you?" Kai says, slipping her hand into mine.

"No need baby, our hearts and souls recognize their other halves."

Kaia beams up at me, before resting her head on my chest, and something in me clicks into place. This is what I've been missing since I was eighteen years old. My other half. My woman. My Kaia.

Kaia

"Um Mom, those soccer women are coming in," Annie-Bella says, eyeing the door as the little bell above it jingles.

"OK baby, I'll seat them in my section," I press a kiss to her head and grab the coffee pot, ready to serve the horrible bitches. It's been two weeks since our kids were kicked off the team, and I have to admit my weekends have been so much nicer seeing as I don't have to fight with them anymore.

"Kaia, how *nice* to see you." Chelsea sneers as her bimbo friends titter behind her. "I heard you moved into that trashy motorcycle club compound. Once trash, always trash, huh?"

"Chelsea, how's your husband's nose? I hope the plastic surgery went well," I smirk, filling up their coffee cups. "What can I get you all?"

"Just the usual," one of the bimbos says. "And can you make sure the berry compote is fresh this time?" More snickering rings out from their table as I walk behind the counter to place their order.

"Five granola's, Marv," I call out, slapping my hand on the counter top to get his attention as the bell above the door sounds out again.

Turning, I'm met with the girl gang, Pops and Mad Dog heading toward the stools up at the counter. "Well, lookie at you all here. What can I get ya?"

"Oh, maybe a round of milkshakes?" Lovely asks, perching on the stool before adding, "And a little revenge," she beams, her cheeks flushed.

Looking around, I lean closer. "What do you know?"

"Oh, nothing yet, but we'll have to wait and see." Remy

winks.

Marv rings the kitchen bell and Annie steps up next to me, helping me with the food for Chelsea's table.

"It'll sort itself out soon enough. It's just a mess up with the insurance, you know how insurance can be," Chelsea says in a voice less confident than usual.

"I don't see why your insurance is refusing to pay for his nose job, but you guys are loaded, so I'm sure you'll just pay for it outright."

Chelsea gives her friend a tight smile and doesn't even spare me a glance when I place her lame granola in front of her.

I move back to my spot behind the counter as the twins circulate around the busy dining room doing top ups or clearing plates.

"Did you do something to Chelsea's health insurance? She said something about them not paying for her husband's nose job," I murmur to the gang.

Pops snorts and then he and Mad Dog chuckle, eyes glinting. Chewy sits stock still, her fingers tapping on the counter top as she stares in the direction of the women. I share a look with Mira, who gives me two thumbs up. Shrugging I go about my business, which today seems to be ignoring the hideous witches cackling in the corner, throwing me and my kids the stink eye.

The sound of motorcycle pipes rumble through the diner and I flick my gaze to the window, watching as the DRMC all pull up, one by one, parking their bikes neatly out the front. I grin as my man comes walking toward me, his big boots stopping when they meet the toes of my sneakers. He grips the sides of the Ol Lady cut he gave me at the party two weeks ago, using his grip to pull me closer and kissing me like he hasn't seen me in years. Much to the disgust of the twins behind me.

"So gross! You saw her this morning, bruh," Jax spits.

"You'll understand one day, son," Leo says, reaching out to ruffle Jax's hair and missing as he dodges away. "How's work,babe? Got space for us? Mama Debs is bringing the kids in too."

Gazing around the diner I wave the MC to the two empty back booths. Leo drops a kiss to my lips, pats my ass and follows his brothers.

"Excuse me, biker whore, we'd like to pay," Chelsea sneers. I have the biggest urge to kick her ass and throw her from my diner, but I do the professional thing. Paste a smile on my face and head over with her check.

She holds her card out for me but before I can grasp it she drops it on the floor with an over exaggerated "Oops!" I growl under my breath, the only thing tamping down my temper is the excited looks on the faces of the girl gang.

Running the card through the till I get a big fat "declined" and my lips tip up.

"Ah, Chelsea, sorry about this, but do you have another card? This one is declined," I call from my place behind the counter, so sweetly it hurts my teeth.

Her head spins so fast she looks like the damned Exorcist. "Try it again!" she barks, rolling her eyes at her friends as they start sharing looks.

"Nope. Says insufficient funds," I smile innocently.

"Burn!" The ginger kid that just walked in with Mama Debs and the big littles yells, drawing attention.

Chelsea goes bright red, hurrying over. "There must be some mistake," she says through gritted teeth. "Use this one!" she huffs, flinging another card at me. She taps her foot impatiently waiting for my response.

My eyes dart to the girl gang, Pops and Mad Dog are all leaning on the counter, staring. Flicking my eyes back to the card reader, again I see the words "insufficient funds" on the screen. Turning it around so Chelsea can see it she lets out a stifled scream, then rummages in her handbag.

Looking behind her I see all her friends are whispering, sharing pitying looks at Chelsea who is having a shit fit on the phone with her husband.

"So, while Chelsea is having technical difficulties, do any of you ladies have money to pay for breakfast?"

A brunette who has a kid with terrible acne gives me a sour look, before handing over her card. I thank her and trip back to my till, trying hard not to grimace at the pitch Chelsea has reached over the phone. I do what I have to with the card, all for the same outcome as Chelsea's.

"Excuse me, sweetheart?" I call out, waving the card in the air, "It seems you have the same problem as your friend here,"

The woman turns dangerously red, snatching up her phone to probably check her banking. I actually have no idea.

"Audit?" Chelsea screeches.

Snorts catch my attention from the counter where my friends, no, my family watch, eyes glued to the scene unfolding.

"Haha!" The ginger kid in the booth with the DRMC kids laughs, pointing at Chelsea and her friends.

"Shut up, you little shit!" Chelsea hisses at him, setting him off even more. The kid throws his head back and laughs his ass off.

"Ma'am, is there a problem here?" Looking up I roll my lips between my teeth trying not to burst into laughter at Fox, standing on the other side of the counter.

Nitro comes to a stop beside him, their new Rose Grove Police

Department badges clipped to their uniforms. Leo had told me that Moss needed backup he could trust in the PD, but I never thought these two would be the guys who stepped up. I guess the DRMC brothers really do take one for the team when they need to.

"Ah, yes, officer-"

"Deputy," Fox says, trying to hold his own laughter in as Nitro rolls his eyes.

"Oh, sorry Deputy -"

"Ellison."

"Deputy Ellison. Yes, those lovely ladies -" I tip my head toward the table where Chelsea's insufferable friends are still sitting, "are causing a scene because there seems to be a problem with their payment. It's causing a disturbance in my diner."

"I see," Fox nods once, sharing a glance with the girl gang.

He and Nitro make moves to talk to the women at the table, but before they can even reach them Chelsea throws her phone at Fox, hitting him in the chest and all the women scatter.

"Wait, are they running from the *police*?" Mira asks incredulously.

"They need to be. All those women are married to men who are embezzlers, ponzi schemers, or just shit at filing taxes," Chewy says before sucking on her milkshake straw. "Won't be long now and everyone in town will know that particular bunch of women are having severe financial troubles."

Mama Debs claps her hands, "Did we film it?"

"Yup," Mad Dog answers, pointing to the booth in the corner where the ginger is standing on the table, cell phone in hand cackling his red head off.

"I may hate that little asshole Rodney, but he sure does have his uses," Pops grumbles.

Looking around the diner I take in the faces of the girl gang, Pops and Mad Dog, the MC brothers in the booth laughing at the chaos, the big littles eating fries and plotting, and my own two, standing behind the counter looking happier and more settled than they ever have before. Then my gaze moves to the man who made this all happen, who gave me my twins and a whole family and I can't help but think how different things could have been if he never walked into the diner asking me to trust him to take care of us.

"You all good there, little mama?" Leo's deep voice washes over me, and I lean into his stupidly hard chest.

"Yeah babe, just happy to be home."

Epilogue

Nitro

"This shit is for the birds," Fox grouses. Again.

"Babe, it's part of the job, suck it up."

"I'd rather be sucking something else," he teases, his dark eyes hooded as he bites his lip.

Fuck, he's sexy. It's damned torture working with him all shift. Made worse by the fact we have to wear these bullshit uniforms which highlight Fox's perky ass. I can feel my cock start to thicken but I'm saved by the radio crackling.

"Dispatch we got a disturbance at Neon Grove, fight in progress,"

Fox groans, banging the back of his head against the patrol car head rest.

"Unit Five responding," I call out over the comms, then make our way two streets over.

The place is full of people much younger and more fun than Fox and myself. Also, wearing much less clothing. It's been a while since either of us have been to this meat market. For a long time this is where Fox and I would come to pick up strange that wanted a taste of both of us. I thought that is what I wanted out of life, just meaningless hookups with my best friend. Then came the attack and I couldn't think of anything I wanted, fuck, needed, more than to let Fox know how I felt about him. How I've always felt about him.

Our sexual relationship with each other may be new, but we always knew, deep down, that to complete us, we needed a third. A woman who could balance out both of our personalities. For me, Fox isn't my best friend or lover, he's one part of my soul. He feels the same, and one day I guess we'll either find the last piece or we'll fill in the missing spaces ourselves.

"Fucking hell, so glad we don't have to come to this shit hole anymore," Fox mumbles under his breath, moving as far as he can from the the roving hands of an intoxicated blonde.

Yelling from near the bar draws my attention, so I hit Fox's arm with the back of my hand, then tip my head in the direction.

"Holy shit," Fox breathes and I know exactly what he's looking at.

The brunette continues to yell at some pale pencil dick in front of her, but it's the back of her that draws Fox's and my attention. Tight pants frame a heart shaped ass and thick thighs, her long, glossy curly hair hitting the small of her back, as if acting as an arrow to that juicy ass. One I recognize immediately.

Stepping up behind her I'm about to open my mouth when she moves like lightning, hitting pencil dick with a flawless hook, right into his doughy face.

When I catch her wrist when she pulls it back to hit him once more, she spins toward us, spitting mad, eyes like fire.

"Jasmine Davies," I can't help the smirk on my face as her

beautiful flushed face stares up at me.

She stares from me, to Fox, then back to me before she blurts out, "I'll do anything if you promise not to tell my brother!"

"That fat bitch broke my nose!" Pencil dick whines, shoving Jazz out of the way, the only thing stopping her from stumbling and falling to the floor is Fox's grip on her.

I roll my eyes and grab pencil dick's arm, roughly leading him toward the exit, Fox, Jazz and Lily who I never saw until now, all following behind.

"How long do we have to do this shit for again?" Fox mumbles under his breath as he blatantly ignores pencil dick's friends pleading his case.

"Another eleven months. Or until we clean out the department."

"Well, we better get on to that."

Epilogue II

Dex

Stretching my arms over my head I try to work out the kinks of riding for the full three and a bit hours it takes to get here. The Keep. It looks a fuck ton better than the last time I was here. The stark buildings somehow look more welcoming, the children playing in the playground area actually look happy, and the women, while carrying haunted looks behind their eyes, seem to have found a semblance of normalcy in their lives for them and their children.

I knew that The Keep works to help those in situations Blanche and her brothers escaped from, but seeing it working first hand is something to behold.

"That large building is the one we decided would be the clubhouse," Vex says, pointing to the building I remembered as housing the meeting hall, and rooms for the council members. Nodding, he continues, "It's been upgraded since the last time you were here. Turns out having loaded sisters helps," he grins.

The rest of my brothers, my men, all flank me as I look toward the new building. Sniper at my right, quietly assessing.

"What do you think, VP?"

"I think this looks like a good place to heal," he murmurs, tipping his chin.

I slap my hand on his shoulder, squeezing. "No truer words have ever been spoken, brother."

I walk up the crushed gravel, coming to a stop on the steps just outside the door to the new clubhouse. Turning, I look to my new club brothers. Some I've known longer than others, but men I'm happy to have at my back.

"Well, DRMC Keep Chapter, welcome home."

My brothers roars ring in my ears as I walk through the front door, my boots echoing on the worn wood, the Pres patch stitched to my chest and a feeling of content settling in my gut. Bring it on.

Thank you for reading!

P hew! I know, it was a LOT!
Please don't forget to drop a review, reviews for authors are like virtual hugs!

If you want to follow me then please drop into any of my groups or social media, I''d love to hear from you!

Friend me on Facebook

Join my group Cleo Browne's Babes

Cleo Browne Books

Rhodie - Devil's Rose MC Book One

August - A Tombs Security + Devil's Rose MC Crossover

Wire - Devil's Rose MC Book Two

Tav Devil's Rose MC Book Three
DRMC - Devil's Rose Merry Christmas

Tank - Devil's Rose MC Book Four

Jules - A Tombs Security + Devil's Rose MC Crossover

Tuesday - Devil's Rose MC Book Five (novella)

Marx - Devil's Rose MC Book Six

Judge - Devil's Rose MC Book Seven

Dima - 31 Days of Trick or Treat
In progress

Fox & Nitro – Devil's Rose MC Book Eight
Coming

DRMC The Keep – Louisiana Chapter
Coming